'Are you suggesting that I actually want you to...to...?'

'Kiss you? That's exactly what I'm suggesting...'

'Then you couldn't be further from the mark!' Alexa snapped, blushing furiously and hating him for reminding her of their kiss, which she would rather have forgotten. 'I'm fine with you being...being attentive when we're out together, but the last thing I want is to be kissed by you! Do you know something, Theo De Angelis? You're the most egotistic, arrogant man I have ever met!'

'I know. I think you told me already. But you make a valid point...just in case...'

She sensed what he was about to do and yet it still took her by surprise, and this time there was an urgency to his kiss that hadn't been there before. His mouth assailed her, his tongue seeking out hers...

The Italian Titans

Temptation personified!

Theo and Daniel De Angelis have never wanted for anything. These influential Italians command empires and conduct every liaison on *their* terms…until now.

Because these enigmatic tycoons are about to face their greatest challenge in the most unlikely of forms— two gorgeous girls with demands of their own!

Find out what happens next in:

Theo's Story:
Wearing the De Angelis Ring
January 2016

Daniel's Story:
The Surprise De Angelis Baby
February 2016

WEARING THE DE ANGELIS RING

BY
CATHY WILLIAMS

First published in Great Britain 2016
by Mills & Boon, an imprint of Harlequin (UK) Limited,
Eton House, 18-24 Paradise Road, Richmond, Surrey, TW9 1SR

© 2016 Cathy Williams

ISBN: 978-0-263-26333-6

Printed and bound in Great Britain
by CPI Antony Rowe, Chippenham, Wiltshire

Cathy Williams can remember reading Mills & Boon Modern Romance books as a teenager, and now that she is writing them she remains an avid fan. For her, there is nothing like creating romantic stories and engaging plots, and each and every book is a new adventure. Cathy lives in London and her three daughters—Charlotte, Olivia and Emma—have always been, and continue to be, the greatest inspiration in her life.

Books by Cathy Williams

Mills & Boon Modern Romance

One Night With Consequences

Seven Sexy Sins

Protecting His Legacy

Visit the Author Profile page at millsandboon.co.uk for more titles.

CHAPTER ONE

'YOU'RE NOT GOING to like what I'm about to say.'

The very second Stefano had called his son and told him that he needed to speak with him as a matter of urgency, Theo had dropped everything and taken the first flight over to Italy, to his father's enormous estate just outside Rome.

Stefano De Angelis was not a man given to drama, and both Theo and his brother, Daniel, had spent the past five years worrying about him. He had never really recovered from the death of his wife, their mother, Rose. The power house who had built a personal fortune from scratch had collapsed into himself, retreating to the sanctuary of his den, immune to the efforts of both his sons to pull him out of his grief. He had continued to eat, sleep, talk and walk, but his soul had departed, leaving only a physical shell behind.

What, Theo thought now, was he about to hear?

Cold fear gripped him.

'Have you asked Daniel as well?' He prowled through the huge sitting room, idly gazing through the window to the sprawling lawns, before finally taking a seat opposite his father.

'This situation does not concern your brother,' Stefano returned, his dark eyes sidestepping his son's piercing green ones.

Theo breathed a sigh of relief. If Daniel hadn't been likewise summoned, then at least a health crisis could be discounted. He had been tempted to phone his brother on the back of his father's summons, but had resisted the impulse because he knew that Daniel was in the throes of a balancing act: trying to close a major deal *and* a minor love affair at the same time.

The deal, his brother had confided several days ago, when he had called from his penthouse apartment in Sydney, was a walk in the park compared to the woman who had been making noises about taking what they had *'one step further'*, and didn't show any promise of retreating without putting up a fight.

'So tell me… What am I not going to like to hear?' Theo encouraged.

'As you are well aware, son…' Stefano's hooded dark eyes gazed off into the distance '…things have not been good with me since your mother died. When my beloved Rose went, she took a big part of me with her.'

'Of us all.'

'But you and your brother are young. I, on the other hand, am an old man—and you know what they say about old dogs and new tricks. Perhaps if her death hadn't been so sudden… Perhaps if I had had time to get used to the idea of her absence…' He sighed. 'But this is not why I called you here, Theo. To moan and complain about something that cannot be changed. I called you here because during the time that I was…shall we say mentally not present, certain unfortunate things took place within the company.'

Theo stilled. His keen eyes noted the nervous play of his father's entwined fingers. His father was the least nervous man he had ever known.

'Unfortunate things…?'

'There has been some substantial mismanagement,'

Stefano declared bluntly. 'And worse, I am afraid. Alfredo, my trusted co-director, has been involved in large-scale embezzlement which has only recently been drawn to my attention. It's a wonder the press hasn't got hold of it. The upshot, Theo, is that vast sums of money—including most of the pension funds—have been hijacked.'

Theo sat back, his lean, handsome face revealing nothing of what was going through his mind.

It was a problem, yes—but a serious one? Not really. At any rate nothing that he couldn't handle.

'If you're worried about the man getting what he deserves, then you can leave that to me,' Theo asserted with cold confidence, his sharp, analytical brain already formulating ways in which payback could be duly extracted. 'And if you're worried about the lost money, then likewise. It will be nothing for me to return what's been misappropriated. No one will ever know.'

'It's not that easy, Theo.'

And Theo knew that now they were approaching the heart of the problem—the reason why he had been summoned.

'I would *never* ask either you or Daniel for financial assistance!' Stefano glowered, his fighting spirit temporarily restored as he contemplated the unthinkable. 'You boys have made your own way in the world and my pride would never allow me to run to either of you with my begging bowl…'

Theo shook his head in frustration at his father's pride—which, he had to concede, both he and Daniel had inherited in bucketloads. 'It would not have been a question of—'

'I'm afraid I went to Carlo Caldini,' Stefano said abruptly. 'There was no choice. The bank was not an option—not when there was a significant chance that they would turn down my request. If that had happened, then the business… Well, what can I say? Everything your mother and I built would have been thrown into the public arena to be picked over by hyenas! At least with Carlo we can keep this between us...'

Theo pressed the pads of his thumbs against his eyes.

Carlo Caldini had once been his father's closest friend and now, for longer than he could remember, was his fiercest adversary. The fact that he had seen fit to go to Carlo for help threatened to bring on a raging headache.

There was absolutely no doubt that whatever his father was going to tell him Theo was not going to want to hear it.

'And what's his price?' he asked, because there was no such thing as a free lunch—and when the lunch was with a sworn enemy then it was going to be the opposite of free.

Exorbitant was the word that sprang to mind.

Stefano fidgeted. 'You're not getting any younger, Theo. You're thirty-two years old! Your mother dearly wished that she would see one of you boys settled... It wasn't to be...'

'I'm not following you...'

'All of this unravelled over eight months ago,' Stefano said heavily. 'During that time it proved impossible to repay the loan. It's been an uphill struggle just picking apart the extent of the losses and dealing with Alfredo...'

'And you kept it all to yourself!'

'There seemed little point in worrying you or your brother.'

'Just tell me what ruinous interest rates Carlo has imposed and I'll deal with it.'

'Here is the part you may not like, son...'

'I'm all ears.'

When it came to money there was nothing Theo couldn't buy, and naturally he would pay the bill without complaint—although he was furious with his father for thinking it necessary to seek help outside the direct family circle.

Pride.

'As you know, Carlo has a daughter. An only child. Sadly there were to be no sons for him.'

Even in the thick of disclosing what he knew his son would not want to hear Stefano couldn't quite conceal the smugness in his voice, and Theo raised his eyebrows wryly. He had never known what had caused the enmity between his father and Carlo, but he suspected that the lifelong grudge stemmed from something ridiculously insignificant.

'What has that got to do with anything?' he asked, frankly bewildered at the tangent his father had taken.

'Alexa... I think you may have met her... Or perhaps not... Well, it seems that the girl is not yet married, and Carlo...' Stefano shrugged. 'He is saddened at that—as I would be had I had a daughter... So part of the repayment schedule—which, in fairness to that sly old fox, is more lenient than at any bank—is that you help him out of his predicament with Alexa. In other words, Theo, I have promised him your hand in marriage to the girl...'

Alexa glared down at the outfit her mother had laid out for her to wear.

Something 'suitable' to meet a man she had no wish to meet, far less marry. A wildly ridiculous frothy dress in startling blue that swept down to the ankles with a plunging neckline and an even more ridiculously plunging back.

She was to be paraded in front of Theo De Angelis like a sacrificial lamb.

She wanted to storm out of the house, head for the nearest port and take a boat to the opposite end of the world—where she would hide out for maybe ten years, until this whole ludicrous situation had been sorted out.

Without her involvement.

At first, when her father had sat her down and told her

that she was to be married to a De Angelis, she had thought that he was joking.

An arranged marriage? In this day and age? To a son of the man with whom he had had a stupid, simmering feud for thirty-five years? What else could it have been but a joke?

That had been a week ago—plenty long enough for her to discover that her father had been deadly serious.

'The poor man is in serious financial trouble.' Carlo Caldini had opened up to her in an attempt to pull at her heartstrings. He had looked at her with a sad expression and mournful eyes. 'True, he and I have not seen eye to eye over the years...'

'All thirty-five of them, Papà...'

'But in the end who else does one turn to but a friend? I would have done the same in his position...'

Alexa had been baffled at this show of seemingly heart-wrenching empathy, but if her father had deemed it fit to rush to the rescue of a man he had spent over three decades deriding, then so be it. What did it have to do with her?

Everything, as it had transpired.

She had been bartered like a...a...piece of meat!

She adored her father, but she would still have dug her heels in and point-blank refused had he not pulled out his trump card—in the shape of her mother.

Cora Caldini, recovering from a stroke, was under doctor's orders to take it easy. No stress, her family had been warned. And, more than that, her father had confided, this last stroke had been the most serious of three... Her heart was weak and all her talk was of her mortality, of her dying before she could see her only child married and settled. What if something happened to her? her father had asked. What if she was taken away from them before her only wish could be granted?

Caught in the eye of a hurricane, Alexa had ranted and

raved, had stood her ground with rousing lectures about modern times, about arranged marriages being a thing of the past. She had pointed out, arms folded, that *they* hadn't had their marriage arranged so why should she? She had waxed lyrical about the importance of love, even though she didn't know the first thing about that. She had darkly suggested that the last thing Cora Caldini would want would be a phoney marriage for all the wrong reasons...

In the end she had gained the only concession that she could. *If* she married the man then it would be on her terms. After a year of unhappy enforced marital misery she would be free to divorce and Stefano De Angelis would be released from his debt. Her father had quickly acquiesced.

Now, with the man due to arrive at their mansion within the hour, she gritted her teeth and returned the elaborate blue dress to the wardrobe from which it had been removed.

She wasn't going to dress up like a doll for a man whose reputation as a commitment-phobe womaniser spanned the country and beyond. There had been no need to look him up on the Internet because she knew all about him—and his brother. Theo and Daniel De Angelis, cut from the same cloth, both ruthless tycoons, both far too good-looking for their own good.

Despite her privileged background, Alexa had made it her life's mission to avoid men like them. She had plenty experience with the superficiality of men who had money and power. She had been surrounded with them for years. She had seen the way they always took it as their God-given right that they could do as they pleased and treat women as they liked simply because *they could.*

She disapproved of everything Theo De Angelis stood for. Certainly the sort of men *she* preferred had always been of the thoughtful and considerate variety.

When she thought about love she thought about her

parents—thought about being swept off her feet by some-one kind and humorous, with whom she could enjoy the sort of united happiness her parents enjoyed. When she contemplated marriage she knew that there would be no compromises made. She would marry her soulmate—the man whose hand she would want to hold for the rest of her life. She had met sufficient idle, arrogant, self-absorbed and vain rich guys—guys *exactly* like Theo De Angelis—to know that she would never find her soulmate amongst them.

And look at her now! So much for all her ideals!

She showered, taking her time because she certainly wasn't going to scuttle down to the drawing room to wait for him—like an eager bride-to-be, thrilled to nab a man the tabloid press had once labelled the most eligible bachelor alive.

And she wasn't going to wear the blue dress—or any dress, for that matter. In fact she wasn't going to wear anything that displayed her body at all.

She chose a pair of jeans and a loose-fitting blouse that was buttoned to the neck and then, taut with suppressed anger at her situation, stared at her reflection in the mirror.

Long, wavy dark hair, pulled back into a no-nonsense bun, framed an oval face. Like her father, she was olive-skinned, with dark eyebrows and thick, dark eyelashes, but from her mother she had inherited her bright turquoise eyes. Her best feature, as far as she was concerned—because the rest did little to excite the imagination. She wasn't long and leggy, and she had stopped being able to fit into a size eight the second she had hit adolescence. Hers, to her eternal regret, was an unfashionable five-foot-four hourglass figure—the sort that personal trainers over the years had tried and failed to whip into shape.

She heard voices before she reached the drawing room

because the door was open, and was assailed by a sudden attack of nerves.

It was one thing pouring scorn on the likes of Theo De Angelis from the relative safety of her bedroom.

It was quite another holding on to her self-righteous, justifiable fury when he was perched on a chair, metres away from her, just out of sight.

She had never seen him in the flesh. He lived in London, but even if he had lived in Rome she probably wouldn't have seen him anyway, because she made a point of avoiding society dos whenever possible.

Heart beating fast, she took a deep breath and entered the drawing room.

Drinks were being served and her parents were sitting opposite him, their body language indicating that they were delighted with whatever he happened to be saying.

Conversation came to an abrupt halt.

Alexa had never thrived on being the centre of attention. Along with her background of vast wealth, she had grown up in circles where the girls were catty and where looks counted for everything. Trapped in a figure that had always catapulted her in the direction of baggy clothes, she had learned to leave the attention-seeking to others, and once she had left school had turned her back on it completely.

Right now she found herself riveted by the long, lean man, relaxing in a deep velvet chair which he seemed to dwarf.

Photos could say so much, but they had given her very little indication of just how big and muscular he was. They had also not prepared her for the sheer outrageousness of his looks. He was drop-dead gorgeous. His hair was cropped short and black, his features perfectly chiselled, his eyes lazy and the most peculiar shade of green she had ever seen, fringed with the sort of luxurious lashes any woman would have given her eye-teeth for.

He was as beautiful as any human being had a right to be...and yet the air of ruthless power that surrounded him like an invisible cloak removed him from being just an incredible-looking man to being a man who drew stares and held on to them.

For a few seconds Alexa's heart seemed to stop and she lost the ability to blink.

But that only lasted for a few seconds and then reality resurfaced, rescuing her from standing there like a stranded goldfish.

Her parents had stood up to make introductions. She didn't take a step closer to him, and neither did he make any move to rush forward. In fact he remained sitting just long enough for her to wonder whether a complete lack of manners was also part of his personality.

'Why didn't you wear the lovely dress I laid out for you on the bed?' her mother whispered, in clear dismay at her choice of clothes.

'I decided that the casual approach was better than showing up in a Cinderella frock. Have you noticed that the man is wearing jeans? I wouldn't say *he* dressed for the occasion, would you?'

She directed a cool smile at him as one of the staff got busy with a bottle of champagne and the business of polite conversation began.

With her parents there some of the pressure was removed, but she still found herself sitting like a rigid plank of wood, back erect, body screaming with tension. When, after half an hour, her parents rose and informed them that they were going out for dinner, she glanced up at her mother with undisguised panic.

'You two should have some time to enjoy yourselves!' Cora chirruped brightly. 'Elena has prepared something, and you can dine informally in the blue room...'

Alexa wondered whether her mother had taken complete leave of her senses.

Enjoy themselves?

Didn't she realise that this was an absolute nightmare? No, of course she didn't. She thought that, yes, it was an arranged union—but one that had been happily accepted by both parties. And she wouldn't have questioned that any further because it was so much what she wanted. Her daughter married and settled.

The door clicked quietly shut behind them and Alexa stared down at her half-drunk glass of champagne. She could feel those fabulous green eyes looking at her, and it infuriated her that he felt he had no need to say anything at all.

'So...' She finally broke the lengthening silence. She glanced quickly at him and just as fast looked away.

'So...' Theo drawled, stretching out his long legs and linking his fingers loosely on his stomach. 'Here we are. I never imagined two weeks ago that I would now be sitting in the Caldini living room, gazing at the excited, radiant face of my bride-to-be...'

What had he been expecting? he asked himself. The fact that Carlo Caldini—a man with more millions than he knew what to do with—had been unable to source a husband for the daughter he clearly wanted married off had said it all.

Plain beyond belief, with an insanely boring personality—that had been the prediction his brother had made, when he had been told about the catastrophe, and Theo had privately agreed. He and Daniel might no longer live in Italy, but they were rich and powerful enough to garner invitations from everyone who mattered, and neither could remember ever meeting the girl—which, along with her failure to be married off, had also said it all.

But, finding himself locked in the jaws of a steel trap,

Theo had determined to make the best of things. Because, however odious the woman was, no marriage was set in stone. There was always a window for negotiation when it came to an out clause, and Theo had already located it.

In the meanwhile he had imagined someone unappealing and terminally shy, who would make a suitable background spouse while his father's company was patched up from the inside. All things considered, he had come to the conclusion that his life would hardly have to change at all. She would remain in Italy, dutifully keeping the home fires burning, he would visit occasionally, work permitting, and she would not complain.

When Alexa had walked into the drawing room he had been startled to discover that she was nothing like the woman he had conjured up in his head.

She was...

He still wasn't entirely sure—and that was a first for him. For if it was one thing Theo De Angelis excelled in, it was an ability to read a woman in under five seconds.

She had sat in mute silence for most of the half hour during which laboured chit chat had been made, with both Carlo and Cora Caldini making sure to tread very carefully around the giant elephant in the room: namely the matter of an arranged marriage.

Cora, he had been told by her husband, knew that the marriage was to be an arrangement, but she knew nothing of the financial situation that had propelled it into existence and nor should she find out. She could deal with an arranged marriage... Several of her friends had children who had been diplomatically set up with suitable partners. It would be tactful not to go into more details.

Alexa's mute silence hadn't translated into the meek subservience he had been expecting.

And looks-wise...

He tilted his head and noted the mutinous, challenging stare she returned.

'And *I* didn't think that I would be sitting here gazing at my devoted and adoring husband-to-be!' Alexa retorted, because there was no reason for her to pretend that this was anything but a fiasco.

Besides, the man was so good-looking that he might just be arrogant enough to think that she actually *wanted* to be in this position.

She felt she should rid him of any such assumption from the start.

'So I'm assuming...' he rose fluidly from the chair to refill her glass with more champagne before topping his up with more of the whisky he had been drinking '...that we're both singing from the same song sheet?'

'What did you expect?' Alexa threw at him, mouth down-turned.

'I could either answer that question truthfully or else ignore it altogether. Which would you rather?'

Alexa shrugged and tore her eyes away from his long, muscular frame. 'We might just as well lay our cards on the table,' she said.

'In which case,' Theo drawled, 'I should tell you I had reached the conclusion that you might be a little desperate... considering Carlo is prepared to throw you in as part of his financial negotiations with my father...'

Slow, furious colour crawled into her cheeks.

'You are the most arrogant man I think I have ever met in my entire life!' Alexa said through gritted teeth.

She gauged the level of satisfaction she would get from flinging her glass at him, but decided that the only way to handle this disaster would be not to let him get to her.

She wasn't going to lose her cool. She *never* lost her cool. It was what made her so good at what she did. She worked in the offices of a group of pro bono lawyers and daily dealt with people in need of practical and emotional help. Three evenings a week she volunteered at a women's shelter. She was calm personified!

'Since we're about to be joined in happily married bliss, I suggest you take that on board and don't think of implementing any changes.'

Theo was perversely enjoying himself, and he put that down to the sort of man he was. The sort who could deal with whatever was thrown at him, however unexpected.

'And in return,' he continued, in the same lazy dark drawl that made her toes curl, '*I* won't try and turn *you* into someone charming and well behaved...'

Alexa glared and bit down hard on the riposte stinging her lips. She had no idea how she was going to survive twelve hours with this man, never mind twelve months.

'I've spoken to my father,' she gritted, 'and he has agreed that we only have to carry out this crazy charade for twelve months. After that we can part company and you can return to your life of— You can return to your life and I can get back to mine.'

Theo wondered what she had been about to say but let it go. He, in actual fact, had secured a far better deal— because *his* twelve months also included a substantial acquisition of Caldini company shares and a seat on the board. It would tie in very nicely with his current diversion into telecommunications.

After the initial shock of the catastrophe that had been presented to him, he had very quickly reached the perfectly correct conclusion that marrying his daughter off was only one benefit for Carlo Caldini in helping his father.

The other was glaringly obvious.

Carlo Caldini ran a juggernaut of a family business but there was no male family member to whom he could leave his legacy—and, like many traditional Italians, he wanted his business to remain in the family. By marrying his daughter to Theo he netted one of the most wildly respected and formidable businessmen on the globe.

And for Theo, Alexa Caldini came with a considerable dowry.

'So no doubt we should be discussing the mechanics,' he said.

'What do you mean?'

'I mean that to the outside world we must be a loved-up pair about to embark on the greatest adventure of our lives. I will not have a whiff of scandal surrounding this, because under no circumstances is my father to be subjected to any manner of rumour about a convenient match concocted to save his company.' His green eyes had cooled. 'Are we one hundred per cent clear on this?'

'Or else what?'

'That's a road I would seriously advise you not to go down.'

His voice was icy cold, with deadly intent, and Alexa shivered. Theo De Angelis had not reached the dizzy heights by being kind and avuncular. He'd probably never helped a little old lady cross a road in his entire life. She wondered how he would react to her world when they were man and wife...

'When we're in public,' he purred silkily, 'you will withdraw your claws. You can keep them for when we're alone together.'

'You might find that you don't like being scratched.' Alexa tilted her chin mutinously and he smiled—a slow, curling smile that did all sorts of weird and unexpected things to her body.

'And *you* might discover that I'm very good when it comes to subduing wild cats.'

Suddenly confused, and feeling horribly out of her depth, Alexa blinked and gulped down the remainder of her champagne.

She might talk the talk, but how good would she be at walking the walk?

She had virtually no experience when it came to the opposite sex. She had been sent off to England to an all girls' boarding school and from there to university, where she had buried herself in books, determined to get her law degree.

Of course there had been a couple of boyfriends, but neither had excited her and she had always been determined to hold out for the Right One—never to sell herself short. They had both cleared off as soon as they'd realised that she wasn't going to hop into bed with them.

Now, as her bright blue eyes tangled with his cool, unreadable green ones, she knew that this was a predator, born to lead and accustomed to obedience.

Obedience she would give him—but only within the parameters that suited them both. If he didn't want anyone getting wind of the real reason for their union she, in turn, did not want to embarrass her parents, whom she dearly loved.

He wanted her to put up a public front and she would—but the second they closed the door behind them there would be no more game-playing.

And suddenly a thought rippled through her that made her breathing quicken.

When the front door closed...what happened next?

It was something that she would have to broach, and she licked her lips nervously because the mere thought of this big, domineering man touching her sent her whole nervous system into instant meltdown.

He surely wouldn't expect them to sleep together! Not when this was a farce—a marriage of convenience...a union in which there would be no love lost!

Her breathing steadied.

Panic over.

He might be arrogant and ruthless, but he wasn't an idiot—and besides, she knew the sort of women he dated because she had seen pictures in some of the trashy magazines she had flicked through while she was getting her hair done.

Tall, blonde women who wore the minimum of clothing and whose full-time occupation appeared to be personal grooming.

'You said that we need to discuss the mechanics of this...this arrangement...?'

'Shall we do that over dinner—?'

'Why? We might as well hash it out now.'

He stood up, blatantly ignoring her interruption. 'I wouldn't like to kick off our joyous life together on the wrong note,' he drawled, strolling towards the door, which her parents had tactfully shut behind him on their way out.

'What do you mean?' Alexa followed him, disgruntled.

'I mean your mother has had a doubtless delicious meal prepared for us. What kind of guest would I be if I disregarded her invitation?'

'The kind that's marrying me thanks to parental pressure?' Alexa muttered sourly.

He shot her a brief look of appreciation.

'Besides,' she continued, skin tingling from that momentary look, 'you don't strike me as the sort of man who gives a hoot what other people think of him.'

She swept past him, breathing in his clean, woody scent and determinedly ignoring its impact on her senses.

'I find that I'm willing to make an exception for my in-laws-to-be...'

'Why are you taking this so calmly?'

It was the first thing Alexa said as they sat down at the table in the informal dining room. The blue room was still big enough to fit a ten-seater table, but places had been set for them opposite each another at one end. As always, it was a full arrangement, with dinner plates, side plates and separate silver cutlery for every course to be served—in this case salad, soup, main course and dessert.

Alexa could not have felt less hungry, and she looked with uninterest as salads were brought in and placed in front of them.

He, she noted, had no problem with his appetite.

'How else do you imagine I should react?' Theo looked at her, and across the width of the table she felt his overwhelming presence all the more acutely.

There was something intimate about eating together, and she could barely concentrate on her salad as the flutter of nerves threatened to overpower her common sense.

She put that down to her healthy dislike of the man.

'Do you imagine that this is a situation I *enjoy* being in?' he enquired coolly. 'My father dropped this bombshell and I find I've had next to no option but to take the hit.'

'I never thought I'd end up in a marriage with someone who would walk up the aisle only thanks to having to take a hit from a bombshell he couldn't dodge,' Alexa said bitterly—and that was the stark truth.

She had never followed the pattern of her friends, who had believed in sleeping around. She had never assumed that marriage was something to be taken lightly because it could be unpicked without too much difficulty if the going got rough. Her own parents had had a long and extremely happy marriage. Her mother, Irish by heritage, had been a gap-year student when she had met Carlo, and theirs had been a case of love at first sight. Which made it doubly upsetting that her father had seen fit to put her in this position. He had taken advantage of a situation and *she* was going to have to pay the price.

'I don't think that way of thinking will pay dividends in this particular situation...' Theo pushed his salad plate to one side and sprawled back in the chair to look at her coolly. 'We've both been put in an unfortunate position and now we have to deal with it.'

'And you're not angry...?'

'Like I said, there's no point in wasting energy on emotions that won't get either of us anywhere. We're going to present the perfect picture of a couple in love. Naturally there will have to be an engagement and a public announcement. Doubtless there will be cameras. You will smile and gaze adoringly up at me.'

'And what will *you* be doing while I'm smiling and gazing adoringly?'

'Controlling the situation.'

'And this so-called engagement is supposed to last... how long?'

'It'll be brief,' Theo asserted with the sweeping assurance of someone who had given the details a great deal of thought. 'We can't wait to tie the knot.'

'And how is this supposed to make any kind of sense?' Alexa demanded. She lapsed into silence as their salad plates were removed, to be replaced with soup. 'Have you suddenly had a transformation and gone from being a womaniser to a one-woman man who's desperate to get married?'

'And *that*,' Theo said in a hard voice, 'is just the sort of approach I am warning you to avoid.' Then he smiled—a slow, lazy smile that made the breath hitch in her throat. 'I never imagined that you were a spitting cat...' he mused. 'Do you think that's the reason your parents think you'll end up on the shelf...?'

CHAPTER TWO

'I CAN'T BELIEVE you just said that.'

Never had a meal seemed so interminably long. Interrupted by the arrival of their main course—a fish casserole—Alexa could only glare at him with simmering resentment. No one had ever riled her to this extent. His air of superior cool got on her nerves and made her rantings seem childish and petty.

'You have no right to say stuff like that! You don't *know* me!'

Theo dug into his food. She might not be his type, but there was a certain arresting quality to her face. Anger suited her, and he was startled at this reaction—because temper tantrums were things he had always actively discouraged.

Her dig about his womanising had annoyed him, and as far as he was concerned what was good for the goose was likewise good for the gander. If she wanted to throw accusations at him, then her shoulders should be broad enough to take it when he threw a few home truths back at her in return.

Not his style, admittedly, but then again since when had he ever been placed in a situation like this? On every single level she was just the sort of woman he would never naturally be drawn to. Physically, she was nothing like the tall, leggy supermodels he dated and, appearances aside, he liked his women to be obliging and accommodating. His work life was intense enough without having to do battle with a woman.

'Aren't you going to eat?' he asked. 'It's excellent. Maybe I'll get the name of your mother's chef... Do you think she would object if I poached him?'

'Elena isn't a chef,' Alexa muttered. 'She's the house-keeper we've had for centuries. And, yes, I think my mother *would* object if you decided to poach her. For your information, I have never considered myself as *on the shelf.* I'm not one of those women who thinks that the be-all and end-all of life is to get married as fast as you can and start having children.'

'I'm guessing that both your parents *do.*'

Alexa pushed her plate to one side. 'There's no point discussing this. What my parents think or don't think... How long before we get married?'

She was forcibly struck by the surreal situation she was now wading through—and by the fact that her contented life had been turned upside down in the space of a few days.

So she hadn't been leading the most thrilling of lives... But it had taken her ages to get used to being back in Italy after first boarding school and then university abroad, followed by a stint in London, where she had worked for a small law company before her mother's illness had called her back home.

She had spent the past year and a half easing herself into a life that felt foreign. Was it any wonder that excitement and thrills weren't high on her agenda? Once she found her feet, she was sure that the slightly zoned out feeling she lived with much of the time would disappear.

She hadn't banked on excitement landing on her doorstep in the form of a forced marriage.

'Max—two months. And, to return to your question

about the plausibility of my settling down at the speed of light... We both need to agree that it's a case of love getting the better of me.' He shrugged elegantly and stood up, tossing his serviette onto the table and prowling through the room as he thought.

Alexa followed him with her eyes. His movements were economical and graceful. He was wearing black jeans, a white linen shirt which was cuffed to the elbows and loafers, and he exuded elegance. He certainly hadn't dressed for the occasion, but he still managed to look every inch the powerful tycoon that he was. He was obviously one of those people who could pull off elegance wearing anything... If he swapped clothes with a tramp he would still manage to look cool and sexy.

'I broke up with my last girlfriend over three months ago—during which time I've been out of the public eye...'

'You're telling me that the press usually follow everything you do?'

Theo paused, leaned against the window ledge, then looked at her and kept looking at her as the dishes were cleared away. He signalled in a barely discernible gesture that they should be left alone for a while, and the door was duly shut as the last dish was removed. The oak table was left with just the wine decanter and a bottle of champagne.

'I'm high-profile,' he agreed. 'I don't ask for it, but it seems that some reporters have little else to do but take pictures of the rich and famous. It's just a fact of life, and I've become accustomed to dealing with it.'

'I would absolutely *hate* that.'

'It's something to which you might find you have to become accustomed—'

'On top of everything else,' Alexa muttered.

Her eyes flickered towards him and she found that she had to tear them away, because he was just so unfairly compelling to look at.

Theo chose to ignore her interruption. He had anticipated someone plain, docile and quite possibly grateful
to be rescued from the prospect of spinsterhood. A traditional Italian woman who would welcome the abundance
of riches suddenly deposited in her lap—because he knew
without a trace of vanity that he was a good catch.

It would have been hard to locate someone *less* grateful
than the girl now glowering at him, and he banked down
a sudden flare of irritation.

'At any rate,' he pressed on, 'no one will raise eyebrows about the timeline, and the fact that at least on paper
this would appear to be the perfect match will certainly
help things along. We both come from prominent Italian
families... I have found the woman of my dreams, someone close to home, and have decided to steer my life in a
different direction... Both families are overjoyed by the
match...'

'Even though our fathers haven't been on speaking
terms for years?'

'All the more touching. Everyone likes a fairy-tale end-
ing.'

'You're so cynical, aren't you?'

'Realistic and practical.'

'And how are we supposed to have met? We don't even
live in the same country.'

'I don't think it will require great feats of the imagination to come up with something.'

Was she going out of her way to get on his nerves? he
wondered. Did she honestly think that *his* life hadn't also
undergone a seismic change? Less than two weeks ago
he had been a free man—free to go where he pleased, to
have whatever woman he wanted. No one was waiting in
the wings, expecting him to put in an appearance. That
freedom had disappeared in a puff of smoke, but was *he*
whining and complaining? No. He was solution-orientated

and, like it or not, plans had to be made so that this pretence could be seamlessly accepted as nothing short of the absolute truth.

'Let's have your thoughts on this,' he said.

An edge of irritation had crept into his voice and, hearing it, Alexa scowled, once again reduced to feeling petty.

'I suppose we could have met here,' she said, a little ungraciously.

'I occasionally *do* come to Italy to see my father. . It's a realistic enough scenario. You happened to be somewhere... Suddenly my life shifted on its axis... If a reporter asks you for details you can always tell him *no comment* and then gaze adoringly at me. Probably safer than getting tangled up in a lie.'

He looked at her glum face, then down to her baggy, unappealing outfit. No doubt she had pointedly dressed down for a confrontation she didn't want, but it was something that would have to be discussed whether she liked it or not. He suspected not, but treading delicately round the issue wasn't going to do.

'Is that how you normally dress?'

'I beg your pardon?'

'Jeans...baggy tops... And what are you wearing on your feet...?'

Alexa looked at him indignantly and stuck her foot out. 'Trainers.'

'Running shoes? To my mind, they're for running. Are you running anywhere? Have you just come from the gym?'

'What are you getting at?' Her voice had risen a notch. His levels of arrogance were in the process of escalating.

'Credibility,' Theo said succinctly. 'We may make the ideal match, and when our engagement hits the news much will be made of our backgrounds, but even the least observant reporter might question the fact that I've fallen head over heels in love with someone who doesn't appear to give a damn how she looks...'

Alexa's mouth dropped open. She contemplated throwing something at him.

'That is the most insulting thing that has ever been said to me in my entire life!'

'It's not meant to be insulting,' Theo informed her drily. 'I'm looking at this situation from all angles and simply bringing one of those angles to your attention. The women I've dated in the past—'

'There's no need to go into that.' Alexa was mortified, and outraged that he should be tactless enough to criticise her choice of clothing. 'I know *exactly* what sort of women you've dated in the past.'

'How so?'

'I've seen the occasional picture in a trashy mag.' She liked the way the words *trashy mag* rolled off her tongue.

'You read "trashy mags"? You surprise me. I thought I might be getting a highbrow intellectual for a wife. I'm disappointed.'

There was a thread of amusement in his voice which she decided to ignore, because it seemed to point to a side of his personality that wasn't part of the package she had conjured up.

'They're the only things to read at the hairdresser,' Alexa told him airily. 'Great big stacks of silly magazines, full of useless gossip. I saw a picture of you in one of them a couple of months ago. A tall, blonde woman was clinging to you as though she might fall flat on her face unless you kept her propped up. Maybe she'd had too much to drink...' Alexa mused, enjoying herself for the first time that evening. 'I hadn't thought of that. But I suppose those society dos usually involve a lot of alcohol. I've been asked to several over the years,' she inserted, truthfully enough, because as the daughter of a prominent Italian family she had occasionally been asked to some event or other in aid of a good cause, 'but I try and avoid them.'

'How virtuous.'

'So, yes, I know that you date tall model-types. A bit like your brother. *He* also pops up in those kinds of magazines, with some drunken supermodel hanging on to him for dear life...'

Theo thought of Daniel and for a second tried to imagine what the mouthy little brunette facing him would have thought of his brother. His brother was the essence of a playboy—which was why he had laughed uproariously when Theo had told him about the situation he was stuck in.

It would have been Daniel's ultimate nightmare, and he had been overjoyed at the prospect of being able to remain free, single and unattached, without having to worry that their father might start making noises about him settling down. One son who had settled down would be plenty good enough.

'I like the way you think the supermodel was drunk...' Theo murmured, temporarily distracted by her digression and thinking that, yes, there was a very high chance that whoever she had seen clinging to him *had* had too much to drink. 'Maybe she was clinging to me because she liked the sensation of being pressed up against me... A lot of women do...'

Alexa blinked and blushed. 'Well...' the conversation had meandered, and she had only herself to blame '...in case you hadn't noticed I'm not six-foot-two and blonde, so you can't turn me into one of your supermodels...'

'You know exactly what I was talking about, Alexa...'

'Do I?' The way he said her name sent little shivers through her, and her eyes glazed over as she tried to fight off the unusual sensation.

'Show up next to me in a pair of jeans, some trainers and

a baggy sweatshirt and people are going to scratch their heads in bewilderment. And show up next to me you're going to have to—because we're going to spend the next couple of months convincing whoever needs convincing that we're a loved-up couple.'

'I have a *job*…' Alexa stared at him in horror.

'I'm not asking you to shadow me twenty-four hours of the day,' Theo clarified. 'In fact I won't even be in Italy for significant periods of time. My work is primarily in London. I will, however, try and arrange my business dealings so that I can be here more often than I normally would. I don't see that I have much choice in the matter. At any rate, when I'm in London you're going to have to drop whatever you're doing and put in an appearance. Two people who are supposed to be madly in love should be madly in love enough that they actually want to spend time in the same country together.'

'Are you telling me that I will have to give up my job?'

Theo looked at her pensively. 'You work in a law office. Am I right?'

'How did you know?'

'Your parents told me before you came down,' Theo said wryly. 'They thought a little background information about you would be a good idea.'

'What else did they say?'

'That you don't seem particularly enthralled by it…'

Alexa was dismayed. She liked what she did well enough, but her liking it only 'well enough' would not have gone unnoticed by her parents. She was their only child, and they could tune in to her moods in ways that were scary.

Was that why they had jumped to the conclusion that she was somehow unhappy with her life?

Like a detective in possession of clue number one, Alexa could begin to see why they might have also come to the conclusion that if she wasn't happy in her job, she wasn't happy in her life—and her mother, traditional as she was, would have instantly decided that it was because there was no guy in the picture. She was now twenty-six years old— at an age when so many Italian girls she had grown up with were married, some with kids. Her mother wouldn't have understood that she was just missing the independence she had had in another country.

'I haven't been there very long.'

'A year and a half is long enough to decide whether you like a job or not. My point being that it won't be any great sacrifice for you to be flexible with it while we indulge in our passionate love affair. And when we do tie the knot it won't be any great sacrifice either for you to jack it in altogether and return to London with me. There's no way I can live out here.'

Alexa's head was spinning. It didn't get worse than this. Not only had her life been overturned, but she felt as if she were on a rollercoaster ride and someone else had complete control of the on/off switch.

'I don't just work at a law firm,' she said tightly, 'I also volunteer three evenings a week at a local women's shelter, and that's something that I *do* happen to like—very much!'

That came as a surprise to Theo. Her parents hadn't mentioned it, and he wondered whether they'd thought it was something he might find a little embarrassing.

He didn't.

In fact he was intrigued. There was no need for her to do anything but enjoy living in the lap of luxury. There was certainly no need for her to have a job, but he could understand her wanting that well enough. However, helping out at a women's shelter was way beyond the call of duty, and he felt a twinge of curiosity about this woman who was going to become his wife.

Since curiosity and women didn't tend to go hand in

hand for him, he allowed himself a few seconds to enjoy the novel sensation.

'Doing what?' he asked with genuine interest.

Alexa hesitated. Determined that total detachment was the only way to deal with a situation she didn't like, convinced anyhow that someone like Theo De Angelis was just the sort of man she could only ever view as an adversary, she was wary of this brief lull in warfare.

He was leaning forward, frowning slightly, his head inclined to one side, waiting for her to reply.

And just for a split second she glimpsed the ferocity of his charm—the charm that drew women like magnets and ensured that his face was always plastered somewhere inside one of those trashy magazines she had told him about.

For a split second it was as if she were the only woman in the universe who interested him. That was how it felt. And even though she knew that it was an illusion, and it didn't change her fundamental opinion of him, she was still...

Sucked in...

'I... You probably don't get this...' she tried for defensive and belligerent but achieved breathless '...but I *am* actually interested in putting back into the community...'

'I'd like to argue that one with you, but go on...'

'I did Law at university, and my experience has been working with pro bono legal teams. I like the thought of being able to help people who need legal aid but haven't got the money to hire some fancy, expensive lawyer. I like thinking that the little guy can get as much from the system as someone with money.' Her voice picked up with enthusiasm. 'One thing led to another, and I found out about a women's shelter that needed volunteers. I thought it would be just the sort of thing I might like—and I do. I help out there on every level...from mucking in with the general work to giving some of the women there legal advice...'

She stopped abruptly, a little embarrassed at the way she had opened up, even though she was hardly divulging state secrets.

'Anyway,' she said, her guard back up and firmly in place, 'there's no need to dress up for my job *or* for my volunteer work—not that I feel comfortable dressing up anyway. You asked me if jeans and baggy jumpers and trainers are the clothes I like wearing and the answer is *yes*.'

Theo didn't say anything for a few seconds. He was still chewing over the picture she had painted of herself and marvelling that he could have been so far off target in his assumptions about this person who had been dumped on him.

Then he shook aside the moment of introspection.

Back to the matter in hand.

'That's as may be,' he said, in a voice that allowed no wriggle room, 'but you'll need a new wardrobe.'

Alexa was happy to fume once again, even though she could see the sense of what he was saying. Who was going to be convinced that he'd fallen in love with a girl who avoided parties and society affairs and whose wardrobe consisted of varying shades of denim? It just demonstrated how far apart they were in everything aside from their backgrounds, and as far as she was concerned similar backgrounds would never be good enough to bridge the gaps.

Thank goodness there was a time limit on this charade!

'And what sort of clothes would you suggest?' she asked politely. 'Do I have a say in what I wear as the radiant bride-to-be, or are you going to take over that aspect of things as well?'

'Would you like me to? I've never been shopping with a woman in my life before, but I'm more than happy to test-drive the experience with you...'

'I'll choose my own clothes,' Alexa said hurriedly as

her head was filled with images of him sitting on a chair in a boutique and looking at her as she paraded different outfits in front of him. Short, over-endowed on the breast front, and lacking in the legs-up-to-her-armpits arena, she could just imagine the comparisons he would make and inwardly cringed.

'And leaving Italy...?'

He let that very important question drop and wondered what ripples it might cause. She was extremely close to her parents. He knew that. Just as he knew that she had returned from working in London post-haste the moment she'd felt she needed to be by her mother's side.

Alexa shrugged. It wasn't a depressing thought. In fact it might be just about the brightest thing on an otherwise nightmarish horizon.

Of course it would entail living with the man now scrutinising her...

Which brought that awkward subject she had shoved aside back to the surface.

What, exactly, would their married life entail? It would be a silly academic question, of course. She wasn't his type any more than he was hers. But she would have to clarify things—draw a line in the sand, so to speak.

'I would want to carry on working wherever I happened to be,' she told him, and he nodded.

'Do you imagine that I'm the sort of dinosaur who would stop you? At any rate...' He shrugged and glanced at his watch, to find that they had been talking for a lot longer than he had imagined. It wouldn't be long before her parents would return. 'At any rate...' he picked up the thread of what he had been saying '...within the constraints of our so-called marriage you would be free to do whatever you wanted to do.'

Alexa nodded, and wondered what sort of woman he would have liked to marry, and what his expectations might have been. Would he have wanted a little stay-at-home wife? She couldn't picture him as a guy who could ever be domesticated. There was something essentially un-tamed about him. She'd been pushed into this, but so had he. He must have had thoughts about marriage and now he was stuck with her—at least temporarily. His life had been equally disrupted and yet you wouldn't have guessed.

She had noted the way he had looked at his watch. So they might be talking business, but it still felt like an insult to be in a man's company and to find him clock-watching because he wanted to get away.

'Fine,' she said crisply. 'In that case I would look for work as soon as I moved to London. Which…er…brings me to… I feel I ought to get a few things straight…'

'Spit it out.'

'This isn't going to be a *normal* marriage.'

'That's somewhat stating the obvious.'

'We probably won't see much of one another, which suits me just fine, and it'll just be for a few months any-way, but during that time I would appreciate it if you didn't bring women to the house.'

Theo looked at her incredulously. '*"Bring women to the house…"*?'

'I know…' Alexa felt addled by the way those cool green eyes were resting on her face, making her feel as though she had made one big, enormous gaffe. Which she hadn't. She was just getting things straight. 'I know that behind closed doors…you know…we will be able to drop the act… But I would rather I didn't have to bump into any of your supermodels on the staircase…'

'You think I'm going to bring women back to the house I will be sharing with you? Put them in the room next door for easy access?'

'You're going to be with me for a year. I expect you will have…needs…so to speak…' Her cheeks were flaming red and she licked her lips nervously. 'And of course,' she ploughed on into thick silence, 'our marriage will be for show only. I mean...there will be no question of us... sharing a bedroom...or anything. I just want to make that clear.' She gave a high laugh. 'Just stating the obvious! So, when it comes to...er...' Her voice petered out and she looked at him in helpless frustration.

'To...er...?' he encouraged.

'You know what I'm saying!'

'You're giving me permission to have sex with any woman I want, just so long as I don't bring them into the house I will be sharing with you?'

'Yes!'

'That's very considerate and generous of you, but I'm not the sort of man who believes in fooling around outside marriage.'

'But it won't be a *real* marriage...'

'Are you magnanimously giving me permission because you want me to respond in kind?'

'I—I don't know what you mean,' Alexa stammered.

His eyes were chips of ice. 'Then shall I spell it out for you? Are you telling me that I can have sex with any woman I want because you want me to tell you that you can do likewise with any man?'

Alexa's mouth dropped open.

'You can drop the innocent act,' Theo said drily. 'I may be older than you, but I don't hark back to the Dark Ages. You're in your mid-twenties, and I'm guessing that you have a boyfriend stashed away somewhere. Your parents didn't mention anyone on the scene, in which case he probably isn't socially acceptable...'

'Not *socially acceptable*?' was all Alexa could parrot in bewilderment.

Of course—he was judging her by *his* standards. A bolt of white-hot fury lanced through her. She clamped her lips

tightly shut and waited to hear where he would go next
with his crazy assumptions.

'If he was the sort of guy you wanted to show off to
your parents you would have trotted him back home for
a sit-down meal and a meet-and-greet evening by now...'

'Because that's what you've done with your girlfriends
in the past?'

'I've always discouraged that.' Theo waved aside her
interruption. 'But we're not talking about me. We're talking about you.'

'So he's "socially unacceptable..."?' She stifled a bubble of hysterical laughter.

If only he knew! But to a man like Theo De Angelis the
thought of being a twenty-six-year-old virgin would have
been unthinkable. It wouldn't even have crossed his radar!
It would never have occurred to him that there were some
people on the planet who actually weren't interested in
jumping into bed *for the fun of it*—people who were willing to hold out for the real thing...people who believed in
love and were willing to wait till they found it before they
had sex. People who wanted to share the precious gift of
their body with the person they truly loved.

'He's not married...?' he mused, for the first time wondering what her social life was like.

His eyes skimmed over her flushed face and, yes...there
was definitely something curiously appealing about her—
something that would definitely be considered attractive
by any number of men.

What would she look like with her clothes off?

Just like that his imagination fired up. Her clothes re-
vealed nothing, but the jut of her breasts suggested that
she had more than a generous handful. Big breasts, with
big nipples.

He frowned and shifted as his libido, dormant since he
had dispatched his last girlfriend, sprang into enthusiastic

life. His thick, hard erection pushed against his zipper and he shifted again, annoyed at the way his body was reacting without his permission.

Hell... He had no intention of complicating an already complicated situation by getting curious about a woman who wasn't his type.

But his body was refusing to play ball and he focused on her face, driving inappropriate thoughts from his head.

'What a relief!' Alexa said with thick sarcasm. 'It's nice to know that you think I have *some* morals.'

Theo's eyes narrowed, because the suggestion was there that what she had he obviously lacked in abundance.

What woman had ever insinuated anything like that to him in his life before? It was outrageous. She knew just how to antagonise him, whether deliberately or not, and it took willpower not to waste his energies rising to the bait.

He wondered whether he had touched upon a sensitive issue. Had he hit a home run without even trying? *Was* there some man waiting in the wings? No matter. He would have to be dispatched—and that was certainly something he wasn't going to waste time apologising about.

'I suppose he's one of your do-gooder pals?' Theo asserted flatly. 'Maybe someone working with you at whatever shelter you work at. Am I right? I don't suppose you would want to introduce someone like *that* to your parents. You might enjoy putting the world to rights, but cut to the chase and you're the only child of one of the most important families in the country. You might be allowed freedom of movement to pursue whatever career you want, but when it comes to settling down don't tell me that your parents wouldn't be alarmed if you chose someone who couldn't make ends meet...'

Alexa didn't know whether to be insulted or amused by his freewheeling assumptions. She certainly wasn't going to set him straight—because why should she? She stoutly reminded herself that whilst it was in her nature to be utterly honest this was a novel situation—there was no need for her to account for herself.

'My parents aren't that small-minded,' she told him with saccharine politeness. 'They wouldn't *care* if I brought home someone who couldn't make ends meet.'

'I beg to differ,' Theo said, in just the kind of tone of voice that set her teeth on edge. 'Why do you think your father is so keen for me to marry you?'

'Apparently because he wants to get me down from the shelf before I take up permanent residence there.' Her cheeks were burning and she was clutching the sides of her chair, leaning forward, every muscle in her body rigid with angry tension.

'He sees me as his natural successor,' Theo informed her smoothly. 'He sees me as the perfect match for you—someone who can run his empire. It's what he wants for you...and of course for himself...'

Alexa whitened. It all made sense now, and she suddenly felt like a pawn caught up in a game that was much bigger than her. Their feuding fathers had sealed a bond and all the players had won except her. Theo's father would have his family name kept intact and his company rescued from the threat of public disgrace. Her mother would have her daughter married and, after her stroke, would have what she had wanted for the past few years. She wouldn't see it as an act of selfishness. Arranged marriages were perfectly acceptable in certain social circles. Her father would likewise see his daughter married off, and in return... Yes, he would have the perfect son-in-law.

And Theo would have...

He didn't have to spell it out for her, because it was obvious now that she was putting two and two together. Theo would wangle part-ownership of her father's company. Maybe not all of it, but his portfolio would increase substantially—not that he needed it.

And she, Alexa, would get one year of gnashing her teeth and trying not to commit homicide.

Right now she could dig her heels in and refuse to go along with what everyone else wanted. But she knew that she wasn't going to do that. She wouldn't stress her mother and risk another health problem which might prove far more serious than the last.

Theo could see the play of emotions on her face as comprehension dawned and he squashed the sickening suspicion that he was responsible for that. She was an adult and she had made her choice. True, she hadn't asked to be put in this unenviable position, but neither had he. Tough situations always made a person stronger, more resilient.

Matter sorted, he said bluntly, 'I know this situation isn't ideal, but if you have a boyfriend he's going to have to go into hiding while we're together. I have no intention of sleeping around behind your back. The press follow me like hyenas and I don't plan on giving them any carcasses to chew on—and you're going to do the same.'

He heard a rustle of activity and the distant sound of voices marking the return of her parents.

'There's an event tomorrow evening.' He stood up and raked his fingers through his hair. 'Formal. I've been invited and you'll be my...guest. It will be our first public appearance together and the perfect opportunity to get the gossip mill at work...'

Feeling as though she had been through several wars and only managed to survive by the skin of her teeth, Alexa stood up as well.

'And of course I'm to dress the part...' she muttered, feeling even more powerless standing in front of him, because he was just so...*big*...

'I intend to stay in the country for at least the next fort-night. There will be several high-profile functions.'

'I'll make sure my wardrobe is overflowing with stuff I wouldn't normally wear in a million years!' she snapped.

Theo smiled slowly. 'I look forward to seeing them… I'll pick you up tomorrow evening at seven. Get ready to be the centre of attention…'

CHAPTER THREE

'DARLING, YOU LOOK BEAUTIFUL...'

Alexa tried hard not to grimace. She had spent a restless night. Her entire mind had seemed to be filled with images of Theo, leaving no room for anything else.

First thing in the morning she had telephoned her boss at work to advise him that she would have to take a temporary leave of absence. She hated leaving him in the lurch, but he would find out soon enough the reasons for her abrupt departure. When pressed, she had only muttered that it was of a personal nature.

Then she had spent the day, at her mother's excited instigation, at various beauty parlours and clothes shops.

She had had her nails done, her face done... She had gone to the hairdressers, where they had trimmed her hair, suffused it with highlights and then insisted she look and admire what they had created... She had traipsed from one shop to another and allowed herself to be guided by personal shoppers...

Alexa knew that it was just the sort of day most girls of her background would have taken for granted. But by the end of the afternoon, laden with bags which had quickly been taken to her room, each elaborate dress carefully hung in her wardrobe while her precious casual clothes had got second billing, she had felt utterly spent.

Now, looking at her mother's thin, beaming face, she

reminded herself why she had embarked on this crazy scheme. Her mother was positively radiant.

She hadn't accompanied her shopping, but had greeted the sight of each purchase with gratifying squeals of delight. Alexa was forced to concede that at long last Cora Caldini had managed to get the doll she had wanted rather than the tomboy she had been stuck with.

'I look…' Alexa stole a glance at her reflection and for a few startling seconds, now that she was seeing the complete and finished product, was lost for words '…different…' she eventually managed to croak.

Neither the mirrors she had cursorily glanced in at the various shops nor the face she had politely and very briefly scanned at the hairdressers seemed to have done justice to the person now reflected back at her.

Different was an understatement, and she was honest enough to acknowledge that.

Her curves were still all there, but for some reason the dress took them, held them, shaped them in some way so that she was…*sexy…*

'I know,' her mother said with immense satisfaction. 'Fabulous! And the colour suits you perfectly.'

That colour was a shimmering pale duck-egg-blue that brought out the brightness of her eyes. Perfectly fitted to slightly below the waist, clinging to her torso like a second skin, the dress flared softly to the ground. The neckline was scooped, but not outrageously so, just affording a tantalising glimpse of the soft swell of her breasts, and the back was equally scooped. When she moved, it flowed in gossamer-fine layers of silk around her, so that every movement she made was as graceful as a dancer's.

The highlights she had ignored at the hairdressers picked up rich copper threads in her hair that she had never noticed. Only a fraction of her hair had been trimmed so that, loose, it tumbled down her back and cascaded over her shoulders.

Her mother had brought in some of her jewellery, and the next half an hour was spent trying on several pieces.

Alexa discovered that she actually enjoyed that half an hour...

She was hardly aware of time passing until there was a knock on the door and she was told that Theo had arrived and was waiting for her by the stairs.

Alexa snapped out of her reverie and smiled at her mother. 'This is the most excited I've seen you in ages. Do you think I should have been going around dressed like this for the past few years?'

'You've never been one for dressing up...' Her mother sighed, still smiling. 'And I wouldn't have changed that for the world. But now and again... Well, my darling, you can see for yourself how wonderful it is to just try something new once in a while. Theo is going to be stunned.'

Theo won't notice what I wear unless I turn up in dungarees and trainers, Alexa wanted to retort as she slipped her feet into stilettoes that were precariously high but absolutely suited to the outfit.

'You're going to be *engaged*—and *married*. Such an exciting time... I know you've been nudged a little in that direction—but, darling, a mother knows best, and I just *know* that the two of you are going to be soulmates. When your father told me that Stefano had mentioned his son had seen you, wanted to meet you... Well, I was over the moon. And, having met him for myself... Well, he's just perfect—and I can tell you feel the same...'

So that's how this little charade is being played out, Alexa thought. Theo had supposedly wanted to set up a meeting with her. Her mother probably had visions of love at first sight, if not at first meeting.

Of course she didn't know of his deal made with the

devil. One year of self-sacrifice and in return shares in their sprawling family company. And, added to that, *his* father's company would be saved from public ruin.

Love and respect for her mother stopped her from prolonging the conversation and hammering the truth home like a battering ram. But it was just so frustrating.

She grabbed a little sequinned bag from the dressing table and then followed her mother along the corridor towards the staircase. Pausing at the top, she looked down to see Theo and her father chatting. Theo's back was to her, but the powerful force of his presence still struck her like a physical blow.

He was dressed as formally as she was. One hand was shoved into the pocket of black hand-tailored trousers, and she could see the pristine white of his shirt-cuff peeping out from beneath his immaculately fitted black jacket.

His body's posture was loose...relaxed. He was a man looking forward to an evening out with the woman he would show off to the world as his wife-to-be.

No wonder her mother thought that the man was the next best thing to sliced bread. Theo had his act down pat. He was so socially adept at handling any situation that anyone looking in would have just seen a prospective son-in-law dedicated to charming his in-laws. Anyone looking in would have probably thought that he had asked her father for her hand in marriage and proposed on bended knee. Which just went to show...

She took a deep breath and began walking down the winding staircase.

Theo turned slowly. Carlo Caldini was proving to be both amusing and intelligent. In fact he reminded Theo of his own father. He could understand why they had been inseparable friends for such a long time. Without much time to spare there had seemed little point in having a drink, so they had remained at the bottom of the staircase, chatting.

It had come as no great surprise that Alexa had not been waiting for him when he arrived. As long as she wasn't hiding out in the broom cupboard in the hope that he would leave without her, then that was all right. He was prepared to wait for as long as it took—whether they arrived on time or not was of little importance to him. In fact the later the better, to some extent, because not only would that limit the hours spent in tedious chatter but it would also ensure that the maximum number of people would witness their arrival, arm in arm.

In Rome, even more than in London, news of the happy couple and their impending nuptials would spread faster than the speed of light.

With his mind toying with the question of how best he could assimilate a wife into his lifestyle without having to alter his day-to-day routine very much, it took Theo a few seconds to focus on the woman gliding with effortless grace down the stairs.

So she'd taken him at his word. He hadn't known what to expect—whether she would actually do what was necessary or else jump aboard her independence bandwagon and don some paint-spattered overalls and hiking boots for the social event to which he had been invited.

Where had that figure come from? She'd hidden it well... With the dress clinging lovingly to her, he could see that she had the perfect hourglass shape. Full breasts narrowed to a slender waist, and even in the floor-length gown he could see that her legs would be shapely. She was the absolute opposite of the stick insects he was accustomed to dating.

Their eyes met and she pursed her lips—just sufficiently to remind him that she was doing this under duress.

If either of her parents had noticed that little show of rebellion they were hiding it well under their broad smiles and proud gazes, but as soon as he had followed her into the chauffeur-driven limousine, Theo turned to her.

'You're going to have to do a bit better than that…' he drawled, making sure that the privacy partition between the driver and the rear seat was firmly up.

She had pressed herself as far away from him as she could physically get without falling out of the car.

'And the evening isn't going to kick off on the right footing if you behave as though I'm carrying the plague,' he went on, keeping his voice even and detached.

'I'll be fine once we get there,' Alexa told him defiantly.

She had noticed that he hadn't complimented her on her outfit. Whilst her father had been holding her at arm's length and showering her with over-the-top compliments Theo had stood back, face impassive. Anyone in that situation would have felt hurt, so it wasn't strange that she had.

Clearly when there was no pressing need to make an impression he wasn't that bothered, so why did he expect her to cosy up against him now? Just in case the driver got suspicious?

'I'm not even sure where we're going,' she said, because yet again his show of good manners had made her feel like a silly kid.

'Art exhibition,' Theo said succinctly. 'Under normal circumstances I would have been in London, but as I happen to be here…'

'An art exhibition…?' She had gone to a couple of those ages ago, with her parents. The art had been incomprehensible and the crowd had been shallow and overdressed.

'There will be no need to stay long,' Theo said mildly. 'Just long enough to create an impression. Although…'

'Although what?' Alexa tensed and looked at him.

In the blue-grey twilight his face was all angles and shadows. She felt a dangerous ripple of response snake through her body and she caught her breath and held it for a few panicked, confused seconds before slowly releasing it.

'Although perhaps we might stay a bit longer than absolutely necessary. After all, it would a shame to waste a dress like that on a forty-minute appearance...'

Alexa was lost for words. He had paid her a compliment, in a backhanded sort of way, and his lazy velvety voice swirled around her like a mind-altering drug. He was leaning against the door, utterly relaxed, and his eyes were broodingly sexy as he watched her, obviously not caring that it was rude to stare.

Of course, she told herself feverishly, what he had *meant* was that it was a dress designed to grab the headlines, so why waste it? Why not stay as long as they could so that it had maximum effect? It hadn't been a compliment directed at her *personally*.

At any rate, it didn't matter one way or the other. This was a business arrangement. They were co-workers, so to speak.

'I've never liked those sorts of things.' Alexa rushed into nervous chatter. 'I think that was the best thing about being away from Italy...not having to go to openings and art shows and film premieres... Not that I was ever forced to, you understand, but I think my parents enjoyed showing me off. The hardship of being the only child of a rich family!'

She was blabbering, but she couldn't seem to stop herself because she knew that if she did she might have to analyse the rush of giddiness that had assailed her on the back of his stupid compliment. And then she would have to link it up with the weird way her body seemed to behave in his presence.

Did it all stem from her lack of experience with the opposite sex?

Blabbering on seemed an easier option than wrestling with those kinds of questions.

'Most people would kill to endure that sort of hardship.'

Cheeks flaming, Alexa turned to look through the window before glancing back at him. The space between them was as big as it could possibly get on the back seat of a very big car, but it still felt tiny. If she reached out she would be able to touch him.

'I get that,' she said stiffly. 'I wasn't complaining. I was talking too much because…'

'Because you're nervous?'

'Aren't you?'

Theo shrugged. He liked the way her hair fell in waves around her. It was much longer than he had originally thought, and it wasn't poker-straight, which seemed to be the only style women below the age of thirty-five wore their hair in the circles he mixed in. A year out from them might be a pleasant break in the monotony. She looked as though she had just climbed out of bed and run her fingers through its length and then left it to its own devices. She was dressed to kill and wearing war paint, but there was still something lacking in artifice about her. She would do those cameras proud.

'Why would I be nervous?'

'Because we're pretending to be something we aren't,' Alexa said bluntly.

'You never did tell me,' he murmured, 'whether you have a boyfriend or not.'

'Because it's none of your business.'

'Of course it's my business,' Theo returned smoothly. Was it? *Really?* Probably not. But he was suddenly curious to find out. 'Reporters will do anything to get background material so that they can flesh out a non-existent story, and you'd be surprised at the efforts they go to to rake up mud. If they uncover a lovelorn pro bono lawyer weeping in a corner somewhere they'll have a field-day. I'm going to have to be prepped with a suitable story.'

'Are you telling me that you're as pure as driven snow when it comes to…to…women? That there are no skeletons in your cupboard that can be uncovered?'

'My love-life is an open book!'

Theo grinned, and she was fascinated at how that open grin could be so engaging. She was as nervous as a kitten and he couldn't have been cooler.

Did *anything* rattle the man?

'We're here.'

Alexa realised that the limo was slowing in front of an impressive white building, fronted with imposing stone columns and a bank of shallow stairs leading up to double doors, which were open. In front of them two uniformed men were checking invitations.

'Boyfriend or no boyfriend?' Theo pressed, circling her wrist with his hand, staying her before she could get out of the car.

'No boyfriend! Okay?'

Theo shot her a smile of such satisfaction that she wanted to smack him. Instead she gritted her teeth and returned his look of satisfaction with one of simmering resentment, which just made him smile a little more.

'No boyfriend. Good. The fewer complications, the better. And stop scowling. Our relationship is too fresh for us to be having arguments in the back seat of a limo. We're still in the honeymoon phase… The way I leave the toothpaste uncovered and forget to put the toilet seat down hasn't started getting on your nerves just yet… So let's smile a lot and face the music…'

He laughed softly at her indignant, helpless expression and gently urged her out of the car as her door was opened for her.

It was a big deal. Cameras flashed at the throng of people clustered outside or making their way in. Even as the car had stopped Alexa had been able to recognise faces. A couple of high-profile politicians, celebrities clinging to other celebrities, as if terrified of moving out of their comfort zones, businessmen in suits, accompanied by wives dripping in diamonds...

Just the sort of crowd she preferred to avoid.

They stepped out of the car and every reporter with every camera seemed to turn, as one, in their direction.

This was the difference between being rich and being rich and newsworthy. The blinding flash of bulbs going off dazzled her, and the steadying arm of Theo, curving around her waist, felt like a solid rock of support in turbulent waters. She knew that she was actually leaning against him. Loathing the man, yet still finding his support strangely comforting.

There was an excited babble of voices and heads turned in their direction.

'You look amazing.'

Theo leant to whisper huskily into her ear and she looked up at him, sensed the popping of cameras taking a picture of their whispered conversation.

'So don't be nervous. I'm right here.'

He felt her automatic protest and his hold on her tightened. He laughed softly under his breath.

'Remember,' he murmured, still pressing close to her, so that no one could overhear what was being said, 'what I told you about retracting those claws in public... Don't forget that we're in love...at the honeymoon stage...you can't get enough of me...'

Alexa had no idea how she managed to deal with the next hour and a half. She drank two glasses of champagne and ate some of the canapés that were passed around. Questions peppered her from various quarters, including from several people—friends of her parents—who wanted to know what was going on.

The gossip mill was in full swing, and they couldn't have announced their togetherness in a more public manner.

Theo didn't leave her side. His arm was around her at all times. She was conscious of that with every step she took.

'Had enough?'

Theo tilted her chin up and their eyes met. Alexa found that she could do little else but stare. His eyes were truly amazing and she felt giddy, sucked in by their green depths. She saw those fabulous, mesmerising eyes flicker and then he was leaning towards her and his mouth was covering hers, grazing it, and then he was delicately teasing his tongue between her lips.

Never in her life had she felt anything like this before. It was as if a series of fireworks had exploded in her head. Every single thought vanished. Indeed, there was no one else in the room—no crowds of people chattering around her, no waiting staff weaving through with trays balanced on hands, no curious eyes boring a hole into her back.

There was just the two of them, and the feel of his tongue meshing with hers, eliciting a soft shudder of response.

Simultaneously the flash of a camera captured the moment, and she knew instantly that Theo had foreseen that.

Everything had been timed to perfection. He had held her with just the right amount of possessiveness, had been attentive to just the right extent, had led the charade, expecting her to follow in his lead—and she had.

They left the still-packed art exhibition and the babble of noise eventually subsided as they moved out into the open foyer outside the room where the main event was taking place, which was far less crowded.

'Well done.'

Theo released her, and without his arm around her reality was re-established.

'What choice did I have?' Alexa asked stiffly as they made their way outside.

The chauffeur had already been summoned and was waiting for them, with the passenger door open and thankfully, no prying cameras to chart their sudden lack of affection.

She was taut with anger. Anger at herself, for having become swept up in that kiss—and not just the kiss. The whispered encouraging compliments...the way he had spent the evening touching her in some way or another... the way he had been the perfect newly loved-up boyfriend.

'About as much as I had.'

The ferocity of his body's response to that well-timed kiss, which would doubtless be in print somewhere by the following morning, had shocked him. He prided himself on being in control of the situation that had been foisted upon him, and he was annoyed with himself for the unrestrained surge in his libido. *Again.*

He propelled her into the waiting car and then slid the partition up so that once again their conversation could not be overheard by their driver.

'Our engagement will be publicly announced in the next few days,' he informed her matter-of-factly. 'So our next bonding session will be at a jeweller's.'

Every trace of affection had disappeared. His cool washed over her like freezing water. He had detached. There was the man who could show one face to the public, and then there was the man who could remove that mask and be someone completely different in private.

This was a lesson she should learn, Alexa thought feverishly. While *her* feelings were all over the place, his had never shifted. He was completely lacking in all emotion—

which was why he had no problem going along with the farce.

Considering she had always thought of herself as a restrained person—someone who could stand back and laugh at the weaknesses of other members of her sex, who got their emotions all tangled up, who ended up being ruled by them—it came as a shock to realise that she wasn't quite the person she had thought herself to be.

She would have to learn fast.

'When shall I pencil that in?' she asked.

'Whenever I tell you to. It will take full precedence over everything else.'

'And I assume there will be some sort of stupid engagement party?'

'I prefer the word *lavish* to *stupid*.'

Alexa glumly pictured the extravagant affair it would no doubt turn out to be. Lots of important people, and among them the friends she had made in her job—who would stick out like elephants in a tea shop.

'I can't see your father having a great time being entertained by my parents,' she said snidely.

'You'd be surprised. They may have their simmering feud, but they have still carried on mixing in the same social circles. You know well enough what it's like over here.'

'Not really. I've spent most of my time abroad. And anyway I never attended those events.' Curiosity got the better of her. 'You've seen our fathers interacting?'

'On a couple of occasions. They bristle in each other's company and yet end up having conversations—like a married couple who can't help fighting but find it hard to stay away from one another. In a room of five hundred people, somehow they'll end up right next to one another. And in between the fraught relations there's usually a fair amount of gossip, which they can't seem to help divulging. Which, in turn, is probably why my father turned to Carlo before heading to the nearest bank. It's a strange case. So I shouldn't worry over-much about your father at our engagement party…it won't be a case of fisticuffs at dusk.'

'Do you know why they fell out?'

'Your guess is as good as mine.'

This lull in hostilities was a temporary soothing balm, but she shook herself free and recalled that this was just a business arrangement with a man she didn't even like.

The limousine was pulling up outside her house, but she remained sitting in the car for a few moments after the car had come to a stop in the courtyard.

'Perhaps you could text me with details of when this visit to the jeweller's is likely to be?' she offered politely.

Theo dragged his thoughts away from the way she was sitting, her body towards him, leaning in so that the soft mounds of her breasts were temptingly on show.

'Let's say I pass by for you at noon tomorrow. The sooner the better, as far as I'm concerned. We can choose a ring and then go somewhere to have lunch.'

Alexa couldn't hide her dismay. 'Lunch? Is that really necessary?'

'Your constant shows of reluctance are really beginning to get on my nerves, Alexa! Yes, *lunch*! What exactly is your dilemma with that? We're newly engaged. Has it occurred to you that as a newly engaged couple we might just want to celebrate together before scuttling off in opposite directions? Scuttling off in opposite directions would be more suited to a couple on the verge of divorce!'

Alexa glared, but this was her life for the time being and she knew that he was right. It was a game that had to be played to the full or not played at all.

She had embarked upon it, and it was too late now to start trying to renegotiate the terms of the contract.

'I can meet you at the jeweller's,' she offered.

'Not good enough. We're browsing together. No need for hiking boots, though…'

'Don't worry,' she sniped in return. 'I know my trainers wouldn't be suitable wear for being seen in public with you.'

'You have to be the most argumentative woman I have ever met in my entire life,' Theo mused in a driven undertone. 'Are you this argumentative with all the men you've been out with?'

Alexa was momentarily caught on the back foot, because the number of men she had dated could be counted on the fingers of one hand and none of them had provoked her the way this man did.

'I've never been out with anyone like you,' she finally gathered enough wit to respond, and Theo grinned.

'Are you telling me that I'm one of a kind?'

'If I'm argumentative, then *you're* downright impossible,' she muttered. 'I should be going in. The lights are on. My parents are probably waiting to hear how our first outing in public went—although judging from the amount of reporters there, they can probably find out in the papers tomorrow.'

'If I've failed to mention it, you handled the evening incredibly well.'

Of their own volition, his eyes dipped to her full and still mutinous mouth.

'Thank you. So did you,' she responded in a stilted voice.

When she glanced down she could see her breasts, too big and too exposed for her liking—especially now that she was in the intimate confines of a car with him—and she surreptitiously adjusted her dress, hoping that he wouldn't notice.

'My mother will ask about this stupid…sorry, this *lavish* engagement party. I expect she'll need time to sort it

out. Could you give me an approximate…er…date? And
I agree with you—the sooner the better.'

Theo marvelled that here was a woman who, only just
engaged to be married to him, was clearly already thinking about the divorce papers being signed. Incredible. The
fact that these were not normal circumstances did little to
assuage his male pride.

'At the outside…a fortnight.'

'Will your brother attend as well as your father?' she
found herself asking, because she knew that his brother
lived on the other side of the world and that during these
transactions he hadn't been a player on the scene.

Theo frowned. 'All bets are off when it comes to that,'
he commented wryly. 'Daniel is in the process of buying
himself a toy, and it may remove him from the scene of
the action while this drama is being played out.'

'Buying a toy?'

'He has his eye on a small cruise ship.'

Much as he loved his brother, Theo was quietly relieved
that Daniel wouldn't be around for the engagement party,
such as it would be. Daniel could be counted on to respond
with nothing but laughter at the fact that his big brother
had found himself tying the knot prematurely. Actually,
tying the knot at all.

'I had no idea that cruise ships could be called *toys*…'
Alexa was distracted enough to say.

'In which case you don't know my brother.'

Alexa thought that that was just as well, because cop-
ing with one was bad enough. Two alpha males didn't bear
thinking about.

She pulled open the car door and stepped out into a
balmy night. Of course he walked her to the door. No pro-
tective arm around her shoulder this time, though! Instead
both hands were firmly thrust in his trouser pockets.

'Isn't your chauffeur going to think that we're not behaving the way two nearly married people should be behaving?' she couldn't help but ask sarcastically, reaching into her bag for the house key, even though she knew that her mother was probably hovering very close to the front door so that she could pounce the second it was opened.

Theo lounged indolently against the door frame, looking down at her as she pulled out the key to insert it into the lock.

'Is that an invitation?' he asked softly.

Alexa raised startled eyes to his.

'What—what on earth are you talking about now?' she stammered, as her wide-eyed gaze was caught and held.

She had the oddest sensation that the oxygen was being sucked out of the air she was breathing as she continued to stare up at him. Her heart was fluttering madly, like a caged bird in a desperate bid for escape.

'What do you think?' Theo asked, in that same soft, lazy drawl that gave her goosebumps.

'Are you suggesting that I actually want you to...to...?'

'Kiss you? That's exactly what I'm suggesting...'

'Then you couldn't be further from the mark!' she snapped, blushing furiously and hating him for reminding her of their kiss, which *she* would rather have forgotten. 'I'm fine with you being...being attentive when we're out together, but the last thing I want is to be *kissed* by you! Do you know something, Theo De Angelis? You're the most egotistical, arrogant man I have ever met!'

'I know. I think you've told me already. But you make a valid point... Just in case...'

She sensed what he was about to do and yet it still took her by surprise—and this time there was an urgency to his kiss that hadn't been there before. His mouth assailed hers, his tongue seeking out hers. He curved a big hand behind her back and pulled her towards him.

He could feel the softness of her breasts squashing

against his chest and knew that he was losing his cool. *Again.* But her mouth was nectar-sweet—and after all, he told himself, it was all for the benefit of a driver who might or might not be taking note. Why take chances...?

'I'll see you tomorrow.' He straightened. 'Engagement ring shopping. Who would have thought...?'

With which he headed back to the car and Alexa, thoroughly unnerved, let herself into the house.

CHAPTER FOUR

As PREDICTED, THE next day the centre pages of all the newspapers had been printed with at least half a dozen pictures of the loving couple. Whoever had taken the photos couldn't have done better when it came to capturing angles that actually seemed to *prove* the lie that they were in love.

Theo's arm was always around her. In several pictures Alexa was looking up at him, mouth parted, the very picture of an enraptured girlfriend—as opposed to wearing the teeth-clenched, resentful expression, which was a lot closer to the truth.

Cora Caldini, who was waiting for her when she emerged at a little after eight, had all the papers spread out on the massive dining room table and Alexa stifled a sigh.

'I know this has all been unexpected for you,' her mother said gently, 'but there's so much to be said for a whirlwind romance—and looking at these pictures...my darling, you *sparkle*.'

Alexa helped herself to coffee and a croissant from the basket of fresh bread on the sideboard. Sparkle? Did minnows sparkle in the presence of hungry, prowling sharks?

'He's certainly a force to contend with,' Alexa forced herself to say. 'And you're right. It wasn't...er...exactly what I had in mind when I thought about meeting the man of my dreams. In fact I'm a little dazed—because he's just the sort of guy I never thought I'd...um...fall for. But... well...life is full of surprises, I guess...'

Unable to be more effusive than that, she scanned the photos once more and wondered whether the reporters had bothered with any other guests at all, or whether they had just decided to trail along behind Theo, snapping pictures.

'Isn't it...?' Her mother beamed. 'And sometimes surprises turn out all the better for being unexpected. It reminds me of when I met your father, as a matter of fact. Of course I'd seen him out and about, but at a distance, and when my parents arranged for us to meet face to face... Well, it really was love at first sight. He was nothing like what I'd expected, and I just fell for that rogue on the spot.'

Always mindful of the consultant's warning words several months ago, in the wake of her mother's third stroke, Alexa reluctantly decided to backtrack.

'Theo's...er...certainly not what I expected,' she conceded. 'I suppose he's quite intelligent, and he has a certain amount of...er...charisma...'

'Funny...your father likes him very much.'

Then perhaps *he* should marry Theo, Alexa thought nastily, surprising herself because she wasn't an uncharitable person by nature.

'That's good.'

'And I know you, my darling. You're as headstrong as I was at your age. If you really didn't like Theo I think we'd all know about it by now! You just don't want to jinx anything—which is why you're being reticent—and I completely understand. It took your father and I ages to have you, and I didn't tell a soul I was pregnant until I couldn't hide it any longer! So I won't press you. Now, tell me what your plans are for today.'

Alexa told her mother and could immediately feel her tummy clench at the prospect of a few hours browsing for a ring and then having lunch in a trendy restaurant with him.

The memory of that blistering kiss the night before had preyed on her mind all night, and she had awoken determined to make sure that they kept a cool distance from one another when there was no one around.

Her thoughts drifted while her mother chatted about rings and reflected on how fast she and Carlo had progressed from that first meeting—marrying within three months and never regretting a day of their long and happy marriage.

Naturally Alexa had known that the man was good-looking. But why did he have to be *so* good-looking? Averagely good-looking would have been all right. She felt that she might have been able to cope with that. But something about Theo De Angelis sparked a reaction in her that burned as fierce as a conflagration.

She didn't understand it. It didn't make sense, And it unsettled her. Scared her, even—although what was there to be scared about?

She surfaced to catch the tail-end of her mother informing her that Theo was going to be dashing off to New York—apparently called away on business. Carlo had wanted to show him around the electronics plant later in the week, talk men stuff, but unfortunately it was a visit that would have to wait.

'He never mentioned that,' Alexa murmured, brightening. 'When? Exactly?'

'Tomorrow, I believe. Your father called him first thing this morning about a visit to the plant and it seems that an emergency blew up overnight. So he wouldn't have mentioned anything to you when you were out.'

'I don't suppose you know how long he'll be away, do you, Mother?'

'A week at the very least... I'm sure he'll be most apologetic when he sees you later and will explain it all himself.

If there's one thing I can say for Stefano's son it's that he's an extremely polite young man...'

Good humour restored on the back of the heartening news that she was going to have a break from Theo, Alexa spent the remainder of the morning looking through her law books, making sure her brain was still ticking over. She dealt with a variety of problems at the shelter on a daily basis, and some of them were practical—questions pertaining to government allowances, retrieving cash from runaway partners, applying for social housing. It paid to keep abreast of the law, and it was no great hardship because she enjoyed it anyway.

At precisely eleven-thirty she got dressed, but she didn't rush.

This time, her spirits light because with Theo out of the country for maybe as long as a fortnight she would at least have some respite from his dangerously incendiary personality, choosing what to wear was far less of a chore than it had been the evening before.

Jeans, but smart black ones, a cream silk camisole top, because it was beautifully warm outside, and flat black pumps. Everything was brand-new, and she was in a good mood when, at twelve sharp, the doorbell rang and she forestalled her mother to answer it.

This time there was no driver, which was even better—because with Theo driving she would be spared those intense, speculative green eyes on her.

'You're in a good mood,' he said flatly, starting the engine of a Ferrari and easing it out of the courtyard towards the buzzing town centre. 'Why does that make me instantly suspicious?'

Alexa relaxed against the passenger's door, her head resting on the window, rolled up thanks to the air-conditioning which kept the temperature wonderfully cool.

She absently noted his strong jawline and the sharp

beauty of his lean face, in profile now as he focused on the road. He was wearing black sunglasses and a navy blue polo shirt and cream trousers. He looked impossibly elegant.

She tugged her eyes away from him, simultaneously deciding that this was just the sort of thing that had to stop—this mindless staring at him—and again applauding the fact that he was going to be away for the next few days. Plenty of time during which she could recover her equilibrium.

'I have no idea,' Alexa said chirpily. 'Doesn't *every* girl like going out shopping for her engagement ring?'

Theo glanced narrowly at her, then relaxed and smiled. 'Indeed. That *would* explain your good mood. You're right. I have yet to meet a woman whose heart doesn't beat faster at the prospect of all things bridal...'

Alexa scowled, because her saccharine-sweet sarcastic rejoinder had clearly backfired. 'I honestly don't think we should waste much time traipsing through shops in search of a diamond ring,' she told him loftily.

'Agreed.' He put the fast car into cruise mode and relaxed in his seat. 'There's no need for us to be seen going from one shop to another in search of the perfect ring. We've already got all the press coverage we need. Speculation is rife that marriage is in the air... If we went to the corner shop and bought a plastic washer it would probably be enough.'

Alexa grimaced as she recalled the spread of newspapers her mother had neatly laid out on the table for her perusal. 'Maybe they'll leave us alone now?' She breathed a sigh of relief at the thought.

'I expect they'll only leave us alone when there's a chunky wedding ring on your finger. Before then there are infinite possibilities for our relationship to crash and burn—and disasters always make better headlines.'

'Why would they assume that it will crash and burn?' How on earth did *real* celebrities survive? she wondered. Without going completely mad? 'And who *cares* if our relationship crashes and burns anyway? Who's interested?'

Alexa was genuinely bewildered, because she might come from a wealthy background but—of her choosing— she was as noticeable as wallpaper. Theo might be similarly rich, with the added bonus of his looks, but he wasn't a *star*...was he...?

Theo shrugged. 'Don't know. Don't care. I just know how the world of media operates and I deal with it. So if you don't want some trigger-happy reporter to shoot you leaving the house without your make-up, be warned.'

'I honestly don't care.'

Theo found an empty space in a crowded square around which designer shops extended outwards in ripples—layers of them, sandwiched between cafés and restaurants. In the centre of the square a trio of mythological creatures figured in bronze cavorted in the centre of an enormous fountain.

He turned to her and said, with utter seriousness, 'You don't, do you?'

'No. Do you?'

'I'm a man. I don't tend to go out wearing make-up. Well, not unless I have to. Sometimes after a long night at work I find a bit of foundation under the eyes...'

Alexa felt her mouth twitch and she grinned shyly and reluctantly at him.

He killed the engine, but she got the impression that there were more questions he wanted to ask her. It felt as if he had been testing her boundary lines...placing one foot over the perimeter of her electric fence, threatening to make inroads. That made her shiver a little.

'Right,' he said briskly. 'Engagement ring.'

In case she started falling behind him he curled his fingers into her hair and pressed his hand to the nape of her neck, gently making sure she kept up with him and slowing his naturally long stride to accommodate her much shorter one.

People turned and looked.

They clearly didn't know exactly who Theo was, but Alexa could almost see their brains churning, trying to figure out why he was famous—because he just *had* to be, looking the way he did.

Something weird rippled through her. A surge of pride. That he was with *her*.

They bypassed the first three jeweller's they came to and went directly to the fourth, which was little more than a nondescript door leading into a shop that was barely visible from the street outside.

'How on earth do you know about this place?'

'You're a woman. How on earth do you *not*?' From behind his dark shades Theo looked down at her upturned face, amused. 'Have you made it your life's mission to avoid leading the sort of life you were expected to lead?'

'I'm not into expensive jewellery. Do you come here with your girlfriends?'

She was acutely conscious of his fingers, still in her hair, absently stroking her neck. It sent shivers racing up and down her spine, and she had to forcibly remind herself just how over the moon she was that he would be disappearing to salvage his business deal and she wouldn't have to put up with these public shows of phoney affection.

Theo paused. 'Quite some time ago a woman I was dating dragged me here and made a point of telling me how exquisite and expensive the jewellery was.'

'So you bought her a diamond ring?' Alexa squeaked.

'Quite some time ago' implied that the woman he had been dating might have been *her* age, and she was struck again at just how sheltered a life she had led—more inter-

ested in her studies than in getting a guy to buy her baubles and trinkets…waiting for love to knock on her door and refusing to spread herself thin in the meanwhile…

'I broke off the relationship,' Theo returned wryly. 'I didn't like the direction it was taking.'

Alexa stopped dead in her tracks. 'You must *hate* this,' she said with sudden force. 'Being trapped into marrying me.'

'The rewards outweigh the inconvenience,' Theo said, fighting an urge to brush the hair blowing softly around her face from her eyes. 'And your dowry is certainly a healthy incentive.'

Feeling like cattle that had been successfully bartered to a new master, Alexa spun round on her heels and pushed open the door to the jewellery shop—which was as unprepossessing on the inside as it was on the outside.

'Take your time,' Theo urged as they were ushered into comfortable chairs and the process of displaying rings began.

The owner of the shop was small, thin and extremely knowledgeable. He seemed to know everything there was to know about diamonds, and tray after tray was brought, with rings nestling in beds of velvet, unpriced and therefore probably priceless.

Since it wasn't a real engagement Alexa didn't care which ring she wore, but it would be ridiculous to choose something that was big and ostentatious.

'What is *your* preference?' She turned to look at Theo, who was lounging in the chair, his long legs stretched out to one side, lightly crossed at the ankles. 'Why don't *you* choose?'

Theo linked his fingers on his washboard-flat stomach and looked at the proprietor with a knowing, man-to-man grin.

'Women!' He shook his head with an expression of rueful indulgence. 'As if *my* opinion would count for anything!'

He stroked her back with one possessive hand and his fingers lingered for fractionally too long on her bra strap. Alexa kept a smile pinned to her face and wriggled a little to dislodge his over-inquisitive hand.

'The women do usually take the lead when it comes to choosing jewellery, sir.'

The proprietor returned Theo's smile and Alexa gritted her teeth as Theo patted her a couple of times on her back and then linked his fingers lightly on his lap once again.

'And this feisty little lady knows that she can have whatever she wants! So what *do* you want?' He looked at her with lazy, sexy bedroom eyes. 'Your wish is my command...'

'If only *that* were true,' Alexa returned pointedly.

She bared her teeth in a smile and hoped that he was sharp enough to read the hidden message, which was along the lines of *If my wish was your command, you would be on the other side of the world...*

Without warning, Theo leaned forward and quickly, but far too effectively, planted a kiss on her mouth.

Their eyes tangled and she realised, heart beating frantically, that he knew exactly what she had been implying and had duly punished her with that kiss.

To add insult to injury, as she returned her attention to the tray in front of her, she felt his big hand rest on her leg and then, shockingly, move upwards, curving over the sensitive skin of her inner thigh and sending a frisson of electric response through her.

Perspiration beaded her upper lip. She snapped her legs shut and pointed to any ring on the tray—she didn't even notice which one she had chosen.

'That'll do!'

Theo's hand on her thigh tightened.

'Perfect choice, if I may say so myself...'

The proprietor reverently removed it from its velvet bed and they listened to his rhapsodies about the purity of the diamond and the rarity of its setting. They were asked to pay attention to the tiny details in the band, which marked it out as a one-off. Alexa was made to try it on. Measurements were painstakingly taken.

The ring cost a small fortune, so it wasn't hard to understand why the whole process was taking for ever.

'That'll do...?' It was the first thing Theo said as they made their way out of the shop.

'Your hand was on my leg,' Alexa said stiffly. And his arm was around her shoulders now. The public face of unity was back in place, although her body was as rigid as a plank of wood.

'Perfectly natural,' Theo purred, giving her shoulder a little squeeze as he guided her to one of the hippest cafés in the area—a place where people went to be seen. 'You're my fiancée. Of course I'm going to want to touch you. Frankly, I can't keep my hands off you...'

It was a load of nonsense, but Alexa still shivered with an illicit little thrill.

Her treacherous mind wondered what it must be like to have this sinfully sexy guy say those words and mean them...

What would it feel like to actually *know* that he couldn't keep his hands off her...?

Her eyes skittered across to him—a quick glance at his face, once again shielded behind his sunglasses. Then, rebelling against all common sense, she noted the width of his shoulders, the lean muscularity of his body, the strength of his forearms and the way his dark hair curled around the dull metal of his watch strap.

She found herself drinking him in and felt her nervous system ratcheting up a notch.

In a couple of days she would be wearing a large diamond rock on her finger. Speculation, such as there was, would be over and she would be officially engaged to the guy now attracting stares from every single woman under the age of eighty and over the age of eighteen.

She was short and unspectacular. He was physical perfection. Even if he did get under her skin in ways that made her want to scream, there was no way that she could deny the sheer beauty of the man.

Was it any wonder that he was taking all this in his stride? He was accustomed to women. A phoney engagement wouldn't faze him and he would be particularly incentivised by the carrot at the end of the stick. He didn't need yet more money, but since when did the wealthy ever turn down the opportunity to add to their bank vaults? *Never.*

As expected, every head swivelled in their direction, and Alexa saw one very leggy blonde disengage herself from her group of friends and make a beeline in their direction.

She stifled a groan.

The blonde stalked towards them, her sharp bob expertly cut and dropping squarely to her shoulders. Even in flats she was close to six foot, and wearing next to nothing. She was rake-thin, flat as a pancake, and had the longest legs Alexa had ever seen—and most of those long legs were exposed because her skirt barely covered her underwear.

Her body language said it all as she chose to ignore Alexa completely, focusing one hundred per cent of her blue-eyed attention on Theo. *Surely it couldn't be true?* The blonde ran her china blue eyes dismissively over Alexa. *The press had it all wrong, hadn't they?*

'I mean, I just can't believe it!' she squeaked, sliding him a naughty smile that was designed to eliminate Alexa from the conversation.

She placed a flattened palm on his chest and shimmied

a little closer. Her hair was so silky and so unbelievably blonde that Alexa could only stare in wonder.

'Andrea...' Theo caught the blonde's hand, halted it firmly in its tracks and held it slightly at a distance before dropping it. It was a gesture that was cool and indifferent. Alexa would have been mortified. The blonde remained perky and upbeat. 'I'd like you to meet Alexa...'

'You're really *short*, aren't you?'

'Alexa is my fiancée.' Theo's voice was soft, silky, glacial. 'And now, before I start getting annoyed at your interruption, I suggest you take yourself back to your group of friends.'

For a few seconds the blonde was nonplussed. Alexa almost, but not quite, felt sorry for her. In her world she would rule supreme, but with a few words from Theo she was reduced to a woman of no standing.

'You don't mean that...'

She tried for provocative and Alexa, with a stab of pure womanly satisfaction, could have told her that she had made a mistake. One look at Theo's shuttered face should have sent the blonde running for cover.

'I mean it, Andrea. I'm giving you two seconds. You don't leave...you see that big guy, standing on the corner...?'

Andrea left, head held high, long, slim body taut with anger and wounded pride.

'I don't mind leaving if you feel that you might be uncomfortable here...' Alexa hovered, uncertain as to what to say in the wake of that dramatic scene.

Theo looked down at her, bemused. 'Why would I feel uncomfortable?'

He signalled with a nod to a hassled-looking waitress, who immediately patted her hair and plastered a smile on her face when she spotted him. Every other customer apparently forgotten, she dashed over to them and cleared a path to a table at the back of the restaurant.

'It's reserved,' the waitress confided with a giggle, 'but I'll sort something else out for the women who reserved it...'

Alexa automatically opened her mouth to protest, but Theo was already sitting and ordering a bottle of wine for them to share without looking at the menu.

'Why do you think I would feel uncomfortable?' he asked again, as soon as she was seated. 'And stop looking guilty because someone else had reserved this table. That charming little waitress said she'd sort it out—let's let her do her job.'

'Her job isn't to pander to customers who haven't booked a table.'

'Not my problem.' He shrugged. 'Now, moving on...'

Alexa sighed. The man was utterly impossible. The more time she spent in his company, the more cemented that impression became.

'I guess that woman must be one of your girlfriends and I just thought it might be awkward for you to be in the same place as she is when you know she'll probably be gossiping about you to her friends...'

Theo was looking utterly relaxed. 'You guess correctly,' he said, pushing back his chair to accommodate his long body. '*Ex*-girlfriend. Barely lasted a month, if you want the truth. The woman turned out to be a bunny-boiler. What started as a little bit of fun with a reasonably attractive woman turned into a dozen phone calls a day and attempts to get into my diary to make sure I wasn't seeing anyone else...'

Andrea had wanted a hell of a lot more than he had been prepared to give. Big mistake. On the love front... he had *nothing* to give. He'd seen what unrestrained emotions did to a guy—had seen the way his mother's death had destroyed his father...the way it had left a great gaping hole in his and Daniel's lives. No. Frothy, dewy-eyed looks from women were the ultimate turn-off to him, and trying to get anything more out of him than passion was their fastest way to the exit.

Alexa's mind had become stuck on his description of the blonde bombshell as a *'reasonably attractive woman'*.

What on earth did he consider *stunning*? Were his values so much different from everyone else's because of the way he looked? What on earth must he think of *her*?

'Some women are possessive, I guess...' she said.

Wine had been brought to the table and poured into oversized goblets and she took a sip of the chilled liquid and then stared at the glass—which seemed less fraught with potential danger than staring at *him* and getting into a mental muddle.

Theo nodded. He found it amazing that a life of luxury and wealth appeared to have had so little effect on the woman sitting opposite him. The privileges which should have turned her into the sort of vain, self-obsessed young woman he met every day of the week in his social circles seemed to have had the opposite effect. Frankly, and against all odds, she roused his curiosity.

'I've always found it a healthy option to stay away from those,' Theo drawled. 'Life's too short to waste any of it with a woman who wants to micro-manage my life. No, I don't give a damn if Andrea is sitting five inches away from us, gossiping with her friends.The only thing Andrea will tell anyone is that I am now engaged.'

'Engaged to someone short.'

He laughed, and his cool green eyes skirted over her flushed face. 'There's no law about falling in love with someone who doesn't fit the insane prototype other people have come up with,' he murmured.

No, Alexa thought, and as he had pointed out they made

the perfect society match. Two prominent families united in marriage. Who would think to scratch beneath the surface to see two individuals who couldn't have been less suited?

'How is it that you have never settled down?' she asked with blunt curiosity.

It was an extremely personal question—but why not? There would be occasions they spent together away from the spotlight, and they couldn't lapse into silence whenever they were together, could they? It would make living together extremely difficult—even if their living together would be taking place in opposite wings of whatever house they ended up living in...

She wondered whether they might not end up being friends, and then nearly laughed hysterically at that notion—because the man was just too *much*, too *larger than life*, to be considered a potential buddy. Potential buddies didn't make you feel as though you were standing on the edge of a precipice, looking down. Buddies were comfortable to be around, unthreatening, safe...

Theo looked at her consideringly. Out of the corner of his eye he could see his ex-girlfriend shooting venomous looks in their direction. He wanted to grin, because he knew that the single thing that would enrage Andrea and all those women like her—all those beautiful, arrogantly self-assured women he had dated in the past—was the fact that he was engaged to someone they would consider downright plain.

The fact that Alexa had been born to privilege would make little difference. Beautiful women were notoriously superficial when it came to judging other women, by standards that were almost always according to looks.

He felt a sudden surge of protectiveness towards his fake wife-to-be.

He reached forward and stroked the side of her face, linking his fingers through hers at the same time.

Another public display of affection, Alexa thought as her heart picked up a frantic pace. And particularly appropriate given that their actions were being minutely watched by an ex-girlfriend who would be busy spreading the news that the most eligible man on the planet had been caught.

An ex-girlfriend who was probably appalled and stunned that he had been stupid enough to fall for someone *like her*...

Alexa had always known that when it came to looks she could only ever aspire to be average. She didn't have razor-sharp cheekbones or long, thirty-four-inch legs or shiny poker-straight hair. She had never felt comfortable in revealing clothes and largely avoided wearing anything that was too bright or too eye-catching.

And yet here she was. Engaged to a man who could have any woman he wanted with the crook of one imperious finger.

Okay, so it might all be pretend, but just for a moment she felt something wicked steal into her. A purely feminine response kicked into gear. His fingers were still entwined with hers and she slowly lifted them to her lips and grazed his knuckles with her mouth.

Heat flared in Theo's eyes. She could almost hear his sharply indrawn breath.

Alexa felt a rush of unfamiliar daring. She raised her eyes to his and held his stare, watched the way his slow smile transformed his face and tried hard not to panic when he leaned in close to her, creating a little bubble of intense intimacy between them.

Nerves threatened to overtake her, but she could feel the blonde's glassy blue eyes boring into her back and that gave her the impetus she needed to lean right into him. To offer her lips to him.

And when he kissed her she responded with an enthusiastic lack of inhibition. She slid her tongue against his and stifled a little moan as, eyes closed, she indulged in naked, forbidden desire.

This was what was expected of her. She was his fiancée. He had confirmed that to an ex-girlfriend, who would have been surprised if they had continued sitting opposite one another making polite conversation. Theo De Angelis was an intensely physical man. You just had to look at him to know that. So kissing him like this, curling her hand into his hair, was only to be expected.

She was just playing the part she had been commissioned to play!

It was liberating to think that she wasn't doing anything out of the ordinary.

It was permission granted to sink into a kiss that was... *explosive.*

When she pulled back she knew that she was shaking a little, and she licked her lips and forced a smile.

'Just for show,' she mumbled, and Theo raised his eyebrows.

'I like it,' he murmured softly. 'I sense a change from all those other displays of affection you didn't seem to enjoy—or was I wrong about that...? Were you actually burning up and looking for a few encores?'

'Of course not!' Her mouth was still tingling from that searing kiss. 'But...'

'But you thought you'd take the opportunity to get one up on the delectable ex-girlfriend who's been shooting you daggers behind your back...?'

'Of course not!' But she blushed furiously.

Theo grinned. 'Trust me, I don't have a problem with your reasoning.'

'I...I hope you don't think that was anything but acting,' Alexa breathed forcefully. 'It's just that you've announced that we're engaged... I thought it would look odd if we didn't act like a newly engaged couple. I mean... you're the one who's kept telling me that we have to make this stupid charade look real...'

'Of course...' He paused, wondering just how real he would like the charade to be. Complications aside... 'And I'm heartened that you're now in such a positive mindset,' he told her, 'because I should tell you that I've been called away on business. I will be out of the country for a week. Maybe a bit less...maybe a bit longer. It's hard to tell because this is a complex deal...'

'I know.'

'You do?'

'My mother broke the news while she was poring over all the pictures of us together at that art opening we attended last night. Don't worry...' Now, more than ever, Alexa was looking forward to a few days on her own—away from his powerful, charismatic personality and the weirdness of their situation. 'I'll make sure to keep the home fires of the newly engaged couple burning...'

'You won't have to do that,' Theo informed her kindly.

'I won't?'

'Don't be silly. How could you think for a moment that I would want you out of my sight for an hour, never mind a week...? No, there will be no need to keep those home fires burning, because you will be right there with me... by my side...'

CHAPTER FIVE

ALEXA WAS APPALLED. She stared at him in open-mouthed consternation, forgetting that her every move was being watched by an interested party.

'Coming with you?' she stuttered.

'Step one in assimilating into my lifestyle,' Theo said smoothly. He leaned back and slouched elegantly in the chair. 'You may hate premieres and art gallery openings, but there will be a certain amount of socialising that you will have to do—like it or not.'

He signalled for the bill without taking his eyes from her face. 'I'm not a fan of meeting and greeting people I have no intention of forming any sort of relationship with,' Theo said drily, 'but it's all part and parcel of the game.'

'Why do I get the feeling that everything about this arrangement is on *your* terms?'

'Explain.'

'Your father is the one who needed a bail-out,' Alexa muttered, feeling terrible at having to remind him of that little detail, because she liked what little she had seen of Stefano De Angelis and was sorry that he, a proud man, had found himself in the position of having to ask for financial assistance from a man he was not on speaking terms with. Although she was beginning to suspect that their so-called feud had petered out into two old men warring through habit over something both had long forgotten about.

Theo's mouth tightened. His father might have taken his eye off the ball, but he didn't need to rehash that misfortune. And he certainly wasn't interested in anyone rehashing it on his behalf.

'He is—but that's old news now. I don't see the point in moaning about what can't be changed.'

'I'm not moaning.' Alexa fiddled with the stem of her wine glass and wondered where all the contents had gone. She'd barely been aware of drinking. Or eating, for that matter. She raised her eyes to his and struggled to look away. 'I just think that *my* life has been completely disrupted while you continue to carry on as if nothing much has happened...'

'Stop feeling sorry for yourself. It makes sense for you to move to London after we are married. I can't conduct my business from here. And remind me... As far as I am aware you don't currently have many ties to this place. You've quit your job and your only other interest appears to be helping at a shelter somewhere. Nothing that can't be left behind at a moment's notice.'

Alexa felt rage rush through her with tidal wave force. If they'd been anywhere but here she would have been tempted to chuck something at him.

How dared he take her life, sum it up and write it off in a handful of words?

But perhaps that was how he treated all women? she thought with scathing distaste.

'Are you like this with all women?' she asked tightly.

'How do you mean?'

Theo frowned, puzzled. How had they gone from a perfectly rational conversation about the dynamics of their married life to some opaque query about his treatment of women? He realised that never before had he had to hold himself to account with anyone—far less a woman.

Her bright eyes glittered as she waited in silence for a response.

Theo raked his fingers through his hair and muttered an oath under his breath. 'I have no idea where you're going with this...'

'It's a simple question,' Alexa said stubbornly.

'I'm extremely fair in my treatment of women,' he said impatiently. 'Exemplary, some might say.'

'Really?'

'Time to go, I think.'

'Only if you answer my question.' She didn't know why it was important to her. She just had a vague feeling that she had to have some say in what was going on or else he would take control of the reins and she would find life as she knew it disappearing even faster than it already was.

'I already have.'

'I feel like you're bullying me.'

Theo shot her a look of pure incredulity. 'I don't believe I'm hearing this!'

'You expect me to change my whole *life*! You don't even bother pretending that I have any say in the matter!'

'I'm cutting through the red tape,' Theo pointed out, with irrefutable logic as far as he was concerned. 'There's nothing you have here that ties you down.'

'What about my parents?'

'Your parents can come to London any time they want,' Theo pointed out. 'In fact I assume they already do, given that your father has business interests there...'

'That's not the point.'

'It's exactly the point—and if you would stop looking at the big picture with irrational feminine logic you would agree with me.'

'Sometimes,' Alexa gritted, 'I really want to hit you.'

'Who knows…?' he replied without hesitation. 'Maybe you will. Although if you do, it won't be in anger…'

'What are you talking about?'

Colour crawled into her cheeks as he raised his eyebrows and shot her a slow, deliberate smile. Her treacherous body tingled. Try as she might, she couldn't bank down the sudden tightening of her nipples, achingly sensitive as they grazed against her lacy bra. And she was aghast to feel spreading dampness between her legs.

'Never tried a bit of bondage?' Theo asked, enjoying the hectic flush in her cheeks. 'I admit I do prefer my women to fully participate in the action—although who knows…? I'm a man who has always been open to new experiences…'

'I've already told you…' Alexa could barely get the words out because her mouth was so dry. 'We won't be… That won't be part of the deal…'

Did she have *any* idea how much he disliked being told that there was something he couldn't do? Theo thought that if she did she might refrain from that approach.

'Anyway, we're straying off the topic.' She cleared her throat. 'I don't like feeling that I have no input.'

'And you're implying that that's the way I treat women generally? You're telling me that you think I'm a bully who takes advantage of women…?'

Alexa cringed because, put like that, it seemed a crazy accusation. If he was a mean bully who took advantage of women why would they care if they were dumped? That blonde who had sidled up to him still had the hots for him. That had been *very* obvious. And she was the sort of woman who could have any man she wanted. If money had been the only thing keeping her in a relationship with Theo, there was no way she would have looked at him the way a starving man eyed up his next meal.

'I'm just saying—'

'I have never bullied a woman in my life before,' Theo interrupted coldly. 'I have extremely healthy relationships with the opposite sex. I am honest to a fault. I have never pretended that commitment and marriage is a possible destination. I have always told them upfront that I'm in it for fun and that fun doesn't last—that beyond that I have nothing to give. But while they're with me they couldn't be treated better. Andrea, as a case in point, was showered with presents and taken to the sort of glittering social dos that have gone a long way to kick-starting her career in film.'

Alexa didn't say anything, because he seemed to expect congratulations for being the sort of guy most women who wanted something other than a ten-second fling would run a mile from. And she was sure that a lot of those women who had been given his rousing speech on not getting thoughts of permanence wouldn't have been quite as cheerful when they were dispatched as he liked to think.

'What do you mean that you have nothing to give beyond *fun*? Why?'

Theo flushed darkly and immediately decided that he had imparted enough information on the subject of his private life. Inside, where the soul stored love, his soul was empty. No reserves left. That place, instead, stored the pain of his father's reaction to loss and the hurt of his own loss…all the result of that big thing called love.

'I'm not laying down laws,' he said snappily, bringing the conversation back to the matter in hand. 'Feel free to tell me if you think it's feasible for me to set up camp here for the duration of our short marriage… Even when you have no strenuous objections to moving to London aside from the fact that it was a decision you feel you didn't reach of your own free will.'

'I've never had anyone make decisions on my behalf.'

She stuck stubbornly to her guns, but she knew that her moral high ground was being eroded from all directions.

'Then maybe you should sit back and enjoy the novelty.'

Theo knew that that remark was tantamount to waving a red rag at a bull with an axe to grind, but he couldn't help himself. Something about the way she reddened and pursed her lips and glared made for addictive watching.

Alexa refused to rise to the bait. They exchanged a brief look, during which a lot seemed to be said without any words passing between them. She communicated with a slight tilt of her chin that she knew exactly what game he was playing—knew that he was trying to rile her because it amused him—and he, in turn, acknowledged the truth in that.

The moment unnerved her.

'I don't like being told what I can wear and what I can't,' she confessed shortly.

'So I'm taking it that part one of your complaint has been dealt with? You're in agreement with me that London would be the best base for us?' He sighed. 'Decisions have to be made,' he said heavily, 'whether you like it or not. Your parents are more than welcome to come and stay with us whenever they want and let's cut to the chase: we'll only be together for just as long as it takes for the ink to dry on our marriage certificate...'

'It's awful. I never thought that I'd end up getting married for all the wrong reasons...'

It was a sobering thought. An arranged marriage—a marriage of convenience—was a marriage without love, and she had always imagined love and marriage as two words inextricably bound together. Yet to some extent her parents' marriage had started on lines very similar to those she was now having to endure.

This tangent threatened to lead them down all sorts of unfamiliar paths, and meandering chat about emotional issues just wasn't his forte, but when Theo looked at the heartfelt expression on her face he found it hard to feel exasperation.

'Love disappears,' he said gruffly. 'And even when it doesn't it burns so strong that it consumes everything around it and ends up self-imploding.'

They were leaning into one another, unconsciously promoting a space around themselves that excluded everyone else in the restaurant, and for that he was glad—because a bride-to-be with a downcast, near to tears expression could in no way be interpreted as a bride-to-be contemplating the happiest day of her life.

As it looked from the outside, they were two people huddled and whispering sweet nothings to one another.

He entwined his fingers with hers and absently stroked her thumb with his to promote the illusion.

'I prefer not to think that way. I prefer to think that you can really find your soulmate and, yes, live happily ever after without everything "self-imploding", as you say. Or else disappearing like water down a drain. That's not how love works. I might be stupid, but I'd like to think that the man for me, the man who can make me happy, is out there...and I'll find him. *We'll find one another.*'

'And who's to say that won't happen...?'

'What do you mean?' For a few seconds Alexa was genuinely disconcerted. Was he talking about *them*? Insinuating that their marriage of convenience could end up becoming the real thing?

'I mean you will move on from me and find this man of your dreams—maybe a little later than you originally planned, and not quite in the order you might have anticipated, but who knows...?'

'What's made you so cynical?' she asked, flabbergasted at the casual way he was happy to dismiss their marriage and divorce as just something a little inconvenient—

something that could be swept aside in the future as though it had never happened.

Whether they were married for twelve months or twelve minutes, and whether she liked him or not, he would leave an impression. She would not be the same person she had been before.

'Let's leave that thorny subject for another day,' Theo told her wryly. 'I'll let you know when we'll be leaving for the States...'

'I didn't say that I was coming with you.'

'Are you going to argue with each and every small thing until we finally part company and go our separate ways? Because if that's your intention it's going to be a very long twelve months.'

'I'm not being argumentative.' She glared at him mutinously and in return he raised his eyebrows in cynical disagreement. 'But if I'm obliged to fall in line and never complain then I think it's only fair that *you* fall in line a bit as well.'

'Are we about to have another bracing conversation about the "separate bedrooms post-marriage" clause?'

'I'd like you to sample how *I* live,' Alexa continued doggedly. 'You want me to go to all sorts of stupid fancy social dos—'

'Don't write them all off. You might find that you actually *enjoy* some...'

Alexa chose to ignore that interruption. 'The least you could do is try and understand what I'll be sacrificing.'

Theo raised his eyebrows and began standing up. He was at a loss to understand what she was talking about. Of course the 'pause' button would have to be pressed on her fairy-tale love and perfect soulmate, but she was young. Plenty of time for her to find that once their committed spell together was at an end.

Frankly, he could tell her that airy-fairy dreams were a

certain recipe for disappointment—but what would be the point of that? She would find out soon enough. She was an enduring romantic, while he...he had about as much faith or interest in romance as a turkey had in signing up for centrepiece duties next to the carving knife on Christmas Day.

She had asked him why he was cynical. He could have told her that he'd had a close-up view of just the sort of pain love could bring—the sort of pain that no one in their right mind would want inflicted on them.

It tended to turn a guy off marriage. Although, in fairness, he knew the day would come when marriage would make sense, and when that day came he anticipated something very much like what he now had—but without the complication of a partner in search of the impossible. Emotions would not take over, leaving him vulnerable to going through what his father had gone through.

Of course he was a very different man from his father. Stefano had met his wife when they had both been young. They had fallen in love when they had both been green around the ears. Theo was anything *but* green around the ears. The opposite. And he prided himself on having the sort of formidable control that would never see him prey to anything he didn't want to feel.

An arranged marriage with the right woman—a woman who wasn't looking for anything that wasn't on the table— would be the kind of marriage he would eventually subscribe to. It made sense.

'Do tell me what that would be. What great "sacrifices" will you be making? Tell me. I'm all ears...'

They were outside now, walking in the balmy sun. He had a case load of documents to read before his trip to New York, but he didn't think that a few minutes prolonging their conversation would hurt.

'I can show you.'

She hailed a cab and leant forward to give the taxi driver

an address. It was on the tip of his tongue to tell her that time was money, but he desisted. Why provide her with another excuse to stage an argument? He had never met a woman as stubborn and as mulish as she was, and those were traits he had no time for. His life was stressful enough, without having a woman digging her heels in and finding objections to every single thing he said or suggested.

'We're here.'

'Here? Where?' The designer shops and smart cafés had been left behind, to be replaced with dingy shop fronts and fast food outlets. It was the sort of place Theo had only ever passed with the windows of his chauffeur-driven car rolled up.

'The shelter where I volunteer,' Alexa told him.

She pointed to a building next to a pawn shop. A grim concrete block fronted by a no-nonsense black door that would have deterred anyone but the most foolhardy.

'I want you to come in and see it—meet some of the other volunteers I work with.' She sprang out of the car, only realising that he hadn't followed when she had slammed the door behind her, at which point she reopened her door and peered inside at him.

'You're not *scared*, are you?' She smirked, because for the first time since she had boarded the rollercoaster ride that had become her life she felt as if she had the upper hand. 'I promise I won't let anything happen to you...'

Theo looked at her, partly outraged because no one had ever dared accuse him of being scared of anything in his life before, partly amused because she had wrong-footed him and not many had done that either.

'What do you think I might be scared of?' he murmured as they headed into the shelter.

'A new experience?' She blushed, hearing the teasing tone in her voice.

'You've broken the ice on that one,' Theo pointed out

drily. 'When it comes to new experiences, you rank right up there as a first.'

'I'll take that as a compliment,' Alexa threw back at him, because she knew that a compliment it certainly hadn't been meant to be.

He smiled slowly, his amazing eyes skirting over her flushed face and doing a lazy inventory of everything else.

'You should,' he murmured. 'I have a jaded palate, and new experiences are always welcome...'

'Even unpleasant ones?'

'What are we talking about, here? The shelter...or you...?'

He was leaning against the door, towering over her, and she felt her heart begin to race. His voice was as smooth as the finest dark chocolate and his eyes were doing all sorts of weird things to her nervous system, muddling her thoughts and stripping her of that momentary feeling of triumph she'd had moments earlier.

She rang the bell and turned away, although she could still feel him staring at her, and suddenly the memory of all those convenient kisses slammed into her, depriving her of breath.

She didn't like him, she reminded herself fiercely. Not only did she not like him—she didn't like the situation she was in.

But he was so sinfully good-looking. He had the sort of face that made her want to stare with helpless fixation and keep on staring. He had that effect on every woman. She had witnessed it for herself. And, whilst she had thought herself immune to that sort of thing, she had to accept the galling truth that she wasn't as immune as she wanted to be.

That was why she found it so unsettling whenever he got too close to her, and why the thought of those kisses kept her awake at night. She was human, and she lacked the necessary experience to deal with a man like Theo De Angelis.

All her old-fashioned ideas about only ever being attracted to her soulmate had been turned on their head...

Which didn't mean that they had disappeared! No, it just meant that she responded to him on a purely physical level, and it was only now that she was accepting that unpalatable truth. She'd always assumed that, for her, physical attraction would only be possible when it was to the guy who had stolen her heart, but she'd been wrong. She could see that now.

Which was a good thing.

Once you knew your enemy, you knew how to arm yourself—and *her* enemy was her treacherous body. She would just have to make sure that she maintained as much distance as she could and never, ever repeated the mistake she had made at the restaurant, when she had initiated that kiss and totally lost herself in it.

It was great that she was going to introduce him to what she did, because it was the one area in which he would be at sea—and that was something she would really enjoy watching.

'You're smiling...' he leant in to whisper as footsteps were heard on the opposite side of the door. 'Private joke or something you'd care to share?'

'Private joke,' she told him promptly.

She looked away as the door was opened and felt a lump in her throat, because she knew that she was going to miss the shelter beyond words when she disappeared off to London.

The prospect of the lifestyle awaiting her there made her want to burst into tears.

Not that *he* would ever understand.

She sneaked a sideways glance at him and, introductions made, took a background seat to watch the spectacle of the great Theo De Angelis fumbling awkwardly in a situation of which he would have had no experience.

He didn't fumble. He charmed all the women there, Franca and Louisa and Marie and Ndali. He introduced himself to some of the women who came to them for practical and emotional help. He pried and prodded into all the rooms and asked so many questions that anyone would have thought that he was an expert on women's shelters.

He talked finance with the guy who ran the place, and made a show of looking at the books. He even went so far as to make suggestions on how small improvements could be made!

She had hoped to watch him squirm, and instead he had dumbfounded her with lots of phoney interest.

'So what exactly is your role there?' was the first thing he asked when they were back outside an hour and a half later.

The work awaiting his attention would have to wait and he had resigned himself to that. Allowing work to take second place to anything was an alien concept to him, but he had watched her as they walked through the premises, watched her interaction with her colleagues, and the casual, friendly, concerned manner with which she had spoken to the some of the women waiting in queues to be seen or chatting to the other volunteers.

Everything about her had breathed open sincerity. Her laughter with her colleagues had been rich and infectious. Frankly, it was the sort of laughter that had been conspicuously absent between *them*, and he had been irked by that.

He had been tolerant of her hostility, even though he privately thought that she should have taken her cue from him and dealt with the whole unfortunate situation with a bit more aplomb—because why rail against the inevitable? And besides, it wasn't destined to be a lifetime situation. He had gritted his teeth at the patently grudging reluctance in her responses to him and the ease with which she accepted as fact the thought that he was deplorable.

But here he had glimpsed a side to her that he hadn't seen before.

It was rare for any woman not to respond to him. Even when he was uninterested in them they still tried hard around him. He had made exceptions for her because of the circumstances of their forced relationship, but only now was he accepting that her indifference was an offence to his pride.

On a more basic level, he wanted what he had seen of her at that shelter. It was human nature to desire the things that are denied. Fact of life.

Alexa was making sure to keep as much distance between them as was acceptable, considering they were supposed to be madly in love. People who were madly in love didn't necessarily have to hold hands everywhere they went—and besides, no one in these streets knew who they were.

Niggling away at the top of her mind was the uncomfortable thought that she fancied the man, and that her plan of seeing him out of his depth and floundering in unfamiliar surroundings—which she had hoped might put the brakes on her stupid attraction to him—had spectacularly backfired.

She should have guessed. He could pull that charm out when it was needed like a magician pulling a rabbit out of a hat.

'Are you *really* interested?' she asked, then belatedly remembered what he had said about her arguing with everything he said. 'Sorry,' she apologised. 'Even if you're not really interested, it's thoughtful of you to pretend to be.'

She was determined to stop letting him get under her skin and rattle her. If she could reach a higher plane of being cool and controlled when she was around him, then her wayward responses could be harnessed and quickly killed off. Fancying someone because of the way they looked was so superficial that it surely couldn't last longer than two minutes.

'And,' she continued, 'you put on a really good show of being interested in what went on there.'

Theo's mouth tightened. Whatever he said or did, she was determined not to give him the benefit of the doubt and it was really beginning to get on his nerves.

'So what exactly is your role there?' he repeated, keeping his voice even and neutral.

They were heading back in the direction of the bars and shops and cafés, looking out for any passing taxis and walking until they could hail one. They had quickly left behind the insalubrious neighbourhood where they had just been, and the houses to either side of them now were well maintained but small and all exactly alike.

Theo realised that this was a part of town he had never actually visited. He wasn't in the country a lot, and when he was his visits were fleeting, because he far preferred to import his father to London.

Having always considered himself a man of the world— widely travelled, the recipient of far more global experiences than most people could ever dream of achieving in a lifetime—he now wondered when and how he had managed to isolate himself so entirely in a very specific social circle that was accessible only to the very, very wealthy. He was delivered to and from places in chauffeur-driven cars, never flew anything but first class, always had the most expensive seats at the opera or the theatre...

Alexa, having come from a very similar background to his own, should have followed the same route—maybe without the high-powered career—but she hadn't and that roused his curiosity.

'It wasn't quite the sort of thing I was expecting,' he expanded truthfully.

'And what *were* you expecting?'

She turned to him and was dazzled by the glare from the sun, which threw his lean, handsome face into a mosaic of shadows. She shielded her eyes and squinted against the sun. Overcome by a sudden feeling of vertigo, she took a couple of small steps backwards.

'A soup kitchen and people waving begging bowls at you?'

She took a deep breath and told herself that sniping and bristling was just a symptom of the stupid attraction she felt for the man, against all odds. If she carried on like that he would begin to wonder why he got under her skin the way he did, and the last thing she wanted was for him to suspect that he got to her, that she was so horribly alert to him.

'I guess *shelter* might be the wrong word...' She fought to inject polite indifference into her words. 'Most people do think of the homeless when they hear the word *shelter*. It's more of an advice bureau. Women come to us with all sorts of problems. Financial, personal... Often we redirect them to other services, but there are people on hand who are really experienced at listening and getting the desperate off the path they've gone down. We also have contacts with companies who offer jobs wherever possible, to help some of them get back on their feet...'

What she had really wanted to show him, Theo mused, were the sort of people she liked. He hadn't been able to help noticing that the men there had been a 'type'.

Caring, soft-spoken, touchy-feely...

Had she subconsciously wanted to show him the sort of guys she liked—was attracted to? Had her intention been to draw comparisons, so that she could underline how far short he fell of her ideal? Just another way of reinforcing her dislike for the position she was in and the man she would be forced to marry—like a Victorian bride being dragged to the altar, kicking and screaming.

And yet…

When she had pulled him towards her in the restaurant and kissed him… Hell, he knew enough about women to know that loathing and dislike hadn't been behind that kiss. She might not want to admit it, but he had felt an urgency there and it intrigued him.

Why wouldn't it?

'Those are the people I enjoy being around,' she carried on, pausing as his driver cruised up alongside them and stopped.

When had he summoned a driver? But of course that would suit him far better than a normal taxi, because there was the option of sliding up that partition so that their conversation could not be overheard. He was always one step ahead.

'Is that your not so subtle way of telling me that those are the sort of *men* you enjoy being around?' He slid into the seat alongside her and predictably slid up the partition, locking them into complete privacy.

Work hard, play hard. Alexa was beginning to understand that, for Theo, the priority was business and after that came sex. He didn't do love and emotion but he did do *sex*. It was why he could be so cool about the situation they were in. He could detach.

'Yes.'

She took a deep breath and thought she had been gifted a golden opportunity to make it perfectly clear to him that those were just the sort of guys she was attracted to. And by attraction she knew that she meant a lot more than just a passing physical tug.

'Their priorities are all in the right places…'

'Heart-warming,' Theo drawled. 'Not the most aggressive of men, though, are they…? One had his hair in a ponytail. I'm thinking that he might be the type to strum a guitar and sing a haunting ballad by way of entertaining a woman...'

'Jorge is absolutely wonderful! Hugely caring! Besides, I don't like aggressive men!'

'And yet your father didn't get where he is by being the sort of man who gets walked over...'

'He's not ruthless...'

'He bartered you in marriage so that he could get *me* as a bonus prize...' Theo pointed out flatly, because he didn't do well when it came to accepting unfavourable comparisons.

'He did it for Mum,' she contradicted. 'I admit he saw an opportunity and seized it, but are you telling me that you wouldn't do the same thing? He's been desperately worried about my mother and he was convinced that her health and her spirits would improve if...if she had *this* to focus on. And that's why I agreed to...to go along with the pretence.'

'And when the pretence comes to its inevitable crashing halt?'

'A year is a long time,' she mumbled, because that thought had occurred to her as well. 'My mother's health will be in a better place and she'll be able to accept that the marriage didn't work out. She'll no longer spend her days thinking that she's on her way out and will die before she sees me settled down.'

'That's *very* optimistic projecting,' Theo declared, in just the sort of arrogantly self-assured voice that got on her nerves. 'She might have a nervous breakdown when we tell her that, sadly, we're joining the statistics of the happily divorced...'

'That's a risk my father was prepared to take and so am I,' Alexa told him sharply. 'Wouldn't *you* have done the same if it had been *your* mother?'

Theo's face closed down. 'I don't deal in pointless hypotheses.'

But it was *just* the sort of solution his father would have hit upon. Deal with today and let tomorrow be a bridge yet to be crossed. And, yes, Theo would have gone along for the ride. He would have done anything for his mother. He and Daniel both.

'All that's beside the point,' he said, and shrugged elegantly. 'Now, our little detour has eaten a chunk of my time. I'm going to get my driver to deliver you to your house and you can pack your bags for our trip to the States. And no protest-packing please...' he added, for good measure. 'During the day you can amuse yourself, but the evenings will be formal occasions. I expect we will be entertained on a fairly lavish scale.'

'Fine—but I insist that we check in to separate rooms,' Alexa told him.

'Already done,' Theo returned smoothly. 'My person in New York has booked us a penthouse suite. Adjoining rooms...'

'But...'

'But what...? Do you think I might try and break down the door between us so that I can ravish you?'

Alexa felt hot colour rush into her cheeks. She had been so intent on laying down her ground rules that she hadn't even considered the obvious—which was that he didn't even fancy her.

'You're getting a little ahead of yourself,' he said kindly. 'Aren't you?'

'I was just...just...making sure... Of course I don't think that!' She thought of the stunning blonde and the nuisance she had eventually turned into and mortification made her skin tingle.

'Then I'll text you our timings and get my driver to collect you...'

They were pulling up outside her house and Alexa felt physically and emotionally drained. She was gripping the door handle before the car had even pulled to a stop.

'Till tomorrow...' he directed at her as she flipped open the door to step out.

Alexa turned and watched helplessly as the car pulled away. A week in New York, where thankfully their time together would be limited, but then would come their engagement party, and then, in short order, a wedding.

By then she would have to make sure that she...

That she was in control...

CHAPTER SIX

ALEXA KNEW WHAT to expect in New York. She had been there several times before and had always loved the buzz of the city that literally never slept.

She met Theo at the check-in desk at the airport, where he was waiting for her, chatting to the woman who had checked him in, who was trying to ignore the fact that there were two other people impatiently waiting in the queue behind him.

'Is that all you've brought with you?' were his opening words as he strolled towards Alexa, who had joined the back of the queue.

Unlike every other woman he had ever travelled with, Alexa had made absolutely no concession to the fact that they would be travelling first class and he liked that. She was in a pair of loose culottes and a T-shirt, with a cardigan lightly draped over her shoulders and flat ballet shoes. There wasn't a scrap of colour in her outfit, and she had braided her long, untamed hair into a neat French plait which hung over one shoulder.

'I have enough for a week—although you haven't mentioned just how long I will be expected to stay.'

In response to that incendiary way of phrasing her question, Theo slung his arm over her shoulder and felt her tense.

'What are you doing?' Alexa squeaked as the line shuffled forward.

'I'm getting you in the mood.'

'In the mood for what?'

'For being my adoring fiancée... And in answer to your question about how long we will be staying...my plans are fluid.'

'What do you mean...?' she asked, hopeful that his 'fluid' plans might entail a reduction in the time they would end up spending in the city. 'Might we be there for less than a week...?'

Alexa looked up at him, eyes wide, and he shot her a half-smile before lowering his head and kissing her—a delicate kiss that feathered over her lips with just the lightest touch from his tongue. He pulled back and turned to the woman who had checked him in.

'Newly engaged,' he explained, giving Alexa a little squeeze so that she was pulled against him.

'How romantic.' The woman eyed Alexa with a look that shrieked, *Lucky you, how did you manage that...?* 'When is the big day?'

She fiddled on her computer, checking her in and ticketing her bag at the same time.

'Not soon enough,' Theo answered on Alexa's behalf. 'The engagement ring is in the process of being altered. Who knows...? We might tie the knot even before the diamond is on your finger—mightn't we, my darling?'

His low, throaty husk made her blood heat and she stared at the woman with a glassy smile.

'Maybe not,' she said gently. 'I don't think my mother would stand for that. She's a stickler for tradition,' Alexa expanded chirpily, 'and by *tradition* I mean taking her time over the wedding arrangements! None of this crazy sprinting up the aisle!'

But then the sooner they tied the knot, the sooner they

would *un*tie it. It wasn't a case of delaying something in the hope that it might disappear altogether if the delay was long enough. No such luck.

'Speaking of diamonds...' Theo told her as they headed towards the first class lounge and away from the chaos of the tax-free shopping area, which was packed.

'*Were* we speaking of diamonds?' Alexa used the pretence of stopping to peer into one of the shop windows to disengage herself from his embrace.

'I've brought something for you...'

He left that teaser hanging in the air as they reached the lounge and were waved through towards a couple of cosy chairs, with a table in front of them on which a few business magazines were fanned out.

'Have you? Alexa looked at him suspiciously. 'What?'

Theo laughed and crossed his legs. 'When are you going to stop fighting me? I've never met anyone with more of an appetite for arguing.'

'As I've told you before—you're the only one I argue with.'

'Sign of a vibrant, lively relationship...'

'It's a sign of two people who don't get along,' Alexa corrected him. 'Which is probably why you've never argued with any of the women you've been out with. And I'm sure they've *all* been vibrant, lively relationships!'

Theo cocked his head to one side and appeared to give her statement a great deal of serious thought.

'Yes,' he agreed eventually, 'I suppose there's been a certain amount of liveliness in the women I've dated...'

'And no arguments,' Alexa persisted, drawn to prolong the conversation and prove a point. 'I can't imagine *any* of your supermodels arguing with you.'

'It's true.' Theo threw his hand up in a gesture that implied rueful but graceful defeat. 'I don't like argumentative women.'

'So it's a good thing that we don't have to like one another, isn't it?'

She had felt just the merest flash of hurt—because who enjoyed being told that they weren't liked? Especially when his job of pretending that he did indeed like and fancy her was so polished and so convincing. And especially when she had grudgingly been forced to concede that she had become just another member of the long list of women who found him physically compelling.

Who wanted to fancy a guy who didn't even *like* them?

Theo didn't bother to get involved further in a conversation he knew wouldn't end up going anywhere, because he was pretty sure that when it came to arguments there was a mighty one brewing like a storm just over the horizon.

It would certainly pay to broach that thorny subject as soon as possible and get it out of the way. Give her the duration of the flight to assimilate and accept.

He grunted something that might have been anything when it came to a response and Alexa banked down a sigh of frustration.

'What is it that you've brought me?' she reminded him briskly.

'I'll show you when we're on the plane,' Theo said, because there could be no available exit door when they were twenty thousand miles up in the air. 'Your bag looks heavy. What have you got in it? Heavy club for beating me over the head?'

'I'm glad you think this is funny,' Alexa told him coldly.

Theo's lips thinned. 'Lighten up, Alexa. Do you take *everything* in life so seriously?'

'This isn't just any little thing.'

'As I've said to you on a number of occasions, it's inevitable—so why don't you just kick back? Or is that something you don't quite know how to do?'

He watched the slow colour crawl into her face. Hard-working, diligent, involved in the caring profession, pointedly making sure to avoid things she considered frivolous... In her own way, it was a statement of rebellion against her privileged background. She had bucked the tide of every other woman in her social circle, who would have settled into a life of pampered predictability and been married by the age of twenty-one to someone not very different from themselves.

The people he had met where she volunteered her services were all very nice indeed, but none of them had struck him as a bundle of fun.

So *did* she ever kick back?

'I kick back.' Alexa heard defiance in her voice.

'Who with? I haven't met the people you used to work with...what were *they* like?'

'Lots of fun,' she told him edgily. 'But you'd probably think they were dull as dishwater.'

'Why?'

'Because they're not the sort of people who think that "fun" is all about nightclubs and being in the public eye.'

'And have *you*? Ever?'

'Have I ever what?'

They were having a perfectly normal conversation, but Alexa still felt as though she was trying to find a foothold on thin ice. Maybe because when she was in his company, try as she might, she never seemed to *feel* normal.

'Thought nightclubs and being in the public eye are fun? Scrap the being in the public eye. No one in their right mind considers *that* fun.'

Although, if he were to be honest, most of the women he had dated in the past had basked in the glare of paparazzi flashbulbs.

'I'm not a nightclub type of person,' Alexa muttered, wondering how the conversation had managed to get here.

'When I meet up with friends we all prefer to go to places where we can actually hear ourselves think.'

Theo had a vision of a group of earnest individuals, solving the problems of the world over cups of espresso. She was positively the *last* sort of person he would ever have been drawn to normally. Frankly, he had little use for people who solved the world's problems over cups of coffee. If the problem was too big to solve, then why waste time talking about it? And if it was solvable then why not just get out there and solve it? Cut out the middle man, which came in the form of pointless discussion.

On the other hand he had watched her in that shelter place of hers—had seen her interaction with the people there and for a fleeting instant had actually caught himself thinking of the supermodels who had graced his arm in the past with a certain amount of distaste.

'And those friends would be your colleagues at work?'

'I've kept in touch with a couple of school friends,' she admitted. Both were married, and one was the proud mother of a baby boy. 'Why are we talking about this anyway?'

She heard the announcement of their flight over the Tannoy. Travelling first class, she knew they would be the last to board the plane, and sure enough, after a brisk ten-minute walk, they were taking their very comfortable seats in the first class section.

'Books,' she said, and Theo shot her a quizzical look as he made himself comfortable.

Flutes of champagne were brought to them and he sipped the drink while he continued to look at her, waiting for an explanation.

'You asked me what I had in my bag. Books. So that I have something to do on the flight over.'

Theo smiled slowly at her and wondered whether her

definition of *kicking back* might involve having some fun on a long-haul flight...

He'd done that once—a long time ago—and had since come to the conclusion that planes were inappropriate when it came to certain activities for a man as big as he was.

Although *private* planes certainly redefined the options...

His thoughts veered off and he held her gaze steadily. 'Books...?' he murmured. 'Let me guess... Non-fiction for the serious reader?'

'Wrong,' Alexa told him triumphantly. 'Romance and crime! Holiday reading...'

'So you're thinking of this as a *holiday*?' He was quick to pick up her stray remark, although he didn't add to that as their champagne was gathered up by a flight attendant and then, mere seconds later, the plane began its ascent. 'Excellent,' he continued heartily, once they were airborne. 'Big improvement on your lack of enthusiasm! A holiday spirit is just the thing.'

It wouldn't last, but he enjoyed watching the way she blushed at the slightest provocation.

He was almost tempted to swing the conversation back to her mission to read books so that he could ask her whether she had ever done anything more adventurous on a plane...with a man...

She might explode with embarrassment.

'I won't be working.' Alexa rushed into hasty explanation. 'So while I wouldn't call it a holiday in the strict sense of the word...'

'Too much detail, Alexa. Let's stick to the holiday spirit theme. But before you dive into one of your books...' Theo sighed and allowed a telling silence to gather momentum until she chewed her lip with sudden anxiety.

'What?'

'There's been a slight change of plan...'

Sudden scenarios flashed through Alexa's head in Technicolor glory. Change of plan? But they were still en route to New York...

But what if New York for a few days was going to expand into other cities across the globe for an indefinite period of time?

What if her one small suitcase with a few essentials ended up being five large trunks to cater for *a change of plan*...?

What if he was going to surprise her with an impromptu wedding so that the baying nosy press could be satisfied?

What if...? What if...? What if...?

The single certainty she had was that she knew she wasn't going to like his change of plan.

He was looking at her with the expression of someone who truly regretted having to say what they were about to say—except Theo De Angelis was immune to any feelings of true regret about anything. Of that she was *very* sure.

'The hotel we were booked into...'

Alexa exhaled a sigh of silent relief, because hotels could always be changed at the last minute—especially when money was no object. And maybe there wouldn't be a penthouse suite available. In which case they would end up sleeping in separate rooms on separate floors. Fingers crossed...

'Don't worry about it,' she told him kindly. 'It's a great hotel, but there are loads of other hotels in Manhattan if for some reason they've double-booked the suite...'

'Double-booked the suite?' Theo laughed shortly. 'Colin Clark wouldn't *dare* do anything of the sort. I'm a frequent enough guest for him to know which side his bread is buttered. Not only have I used that suite on a number of occasions, I have frequently rented it for members of my staff and have held several conferences at the hotel. No... I'm a valued and cherished customer—as I've been told in the past. And *as* a valued and cherished customer, I know that suite will always be available for my use.'

'Then what's the change of plan?'

'Brace yourself...'

They were briefly interrupted by yet more drinks, and a menu which Alexa didn't even look at.

'My brother is going to be in that part of the world...'

'Your brother? Daniel?'

'Special detour before he buys his toy,' Theo informed her drily. 'So that he can meet the radiant bride-to-be...'

'But he knows that— Well, there won't be any need for us to pretend around *him*, will there?'

Alexa had banked on exploring the art galleries on her own during the day and getting through the evenings as best she could. The pressure to be loved-up would not be nearly so intense as it had been at home, because who in New York really cared?

With Theo's brother on the scene she would have to re-sign herself to a little more than mere polite conversation with people she had no intention of ever seeing again. But no matter. In truth, she was curious about his brother— curious to see whether it really *was* possible for two alpha males to be brothers...

She shrugged and rested back, half closing her eyes. Strangely, she could still see Theo's lean, dynamic face, even though her eyes were closed.

His image was imprinted on her retina with the force of a branding iron. No good fighting it. Sooner or later, once she became accustomed to the inconvenience of fan-cying the man, indifference would begin to trickle in, and before she knew it she would be able to look at him with-out a flicker of emotion. He would be just someone she'd happened to share space with for a short period of time— much to her mother's joy and delight.

'Will he be working with you?'

'Oh, no...' Theo drawled. 'My brother is as successful as I am, but his area of expertise is not mine.'

Alexa turned and looked at him. 'You mean *you* wouldn't think about buying a cruise ship as a toy?'

Theo grinned. 'I'm more of a financial guy,' he said. 'I enjoy numbers. Daniel likes the leisure side of things. If he weren't such a successful businessman in the leisure industry there's a strong possibility he would be a beach bum somewhere hot.'

Alexa heard the warmth in Theo's voice and realised that he was in exactly the same position as she was. A devoted child from a close-knit family, willing to make a ridiculously huge sacrifice for the sake of a parent or, in her case, *parents*.

It had been so much easier to pigeonhole him as a one-dimensional cardboard cut-out, and she was shaken at the tangent her thoughts had taken.

'So he'll be there? No big deal.' She closed her eyes once more and tried to block out the silent fizz of electricity radiating from his body.

'Indeed. He will be staying for a matter of just one night, but not, it would only be fair to tell you, at the hotel...'

'That's a shame.' Alexa couldn't stop herself from being just a tiny bit sarcastic. 'You'd think that as you're a *valued and cherished* customer, they would be able to rustle up a room for your brother.'

'Oh, I'm sure they would—if I asked...'

Eyes still closed, Alexa allowed herself a smug little smile. 'But you'd rather he stayed somewhere else? I guess, however close you might be to a sibling, there's still always a part of you that doesn't want them in your pocket...'

'*Not* really where I was going with this conversation,' Theo murmured. 'And, before we get lost in a series of misunderstandings, you should know that Daniel will be staying exactly where *we* will be staying. It just isn't going to be at the hotel, as originally planned…'

Alexa's eyes flew open and she sat up and looked at him. 'Okay… So…?'

'So we'll be going to The Hamptons instead,' Theo told her bluntly. 'Bob, a mutual friend of ours, has something of a mansion there, and I've been persuaded to take him up on his offer to accommodate us…'

'What? *Why?* When did this happen?'

Theo waved his hand in a soothing manner and she only just resisted slapping it away.

Her thoughts were swirling all over the place. None of them were comfortable or pleasant. What was going to happen to her time out, browsing the art galleries, if she was closeted in a house out in The Hamptons? What was going to happen to the peace and quiet she knew she would need just to deal with the wretched man every evening?

She felt physically sick at the unfolding and newly altered scenario.

'Got the call last night. Arrangements were sprung on me. What can a guy do?'

'A guy could have picked up the telephone and called to let me know of the change of plan!' Alexa snapped.

'And risk you bailing on me? No chance. It would have looked very suspect indeed if my beloved fiancée couldn't be bothered to meet her potential brother-in-law, her fiancé's best friend and three top clients who will all be adjusting their schedules for flying visits to the Hamptons to sort out the deal I'm going across to nail…'

'You've told *all of them* that we're engaged…?'

'It would have been peculiar to keep such momentous news to myself—and besides, who knows how far the news has already travelled? You would be surprised how small a world it is, with the internet and Facebook. It would have been downright discourteous for news of my engagement to reach their ears via a third party.'

'I don't have Facebook,' Alexa muttered, feeling well and truly trapped.

'Nor do I. But you can bet that we're in a minority… Bob's wife, Felicity, almost certainly *is* on Facebook—to keep in touch with their daughter in Australia.'

'What am I going to do with myself all day for days on end in a house with people I've never met in my life before?' Alexa was on the verge of undignified sobbing. 'It's just not *fair* that you couldn't even be bothered to tell me until we were in the air…'

'It will be fine,' Theo said. 'Although you might have to adjust your wardrobe a little bit…'

'Meaning…?'

'Those smart outfits might not be appropriate for a house visit.'

'I just can't believe you've done this to me.'

'Let's move on from that. It will be hot in The Hamptons. Outdoor eating is probably going to be the order of the day. Formal long dresses won't work. There's also a swimming pool, and I'm guessing that you didn't pack any swimwear…'

In actual fact Alexa *had* packed a bikini. There was a rooftop pool at the hotel, and she had intended to make use of it during the day when she wasn't out and about busying herself. She hadn't banked on parading in it in front of Theo, and she certainly, even in her wildest nightmares, hadn't envisaged staying at a private house, where she would be expected to hang around a pool with the rest of the guests in nothing but a sheer sarong and the bikini.

'Before we head to Bob's place we can fit in a whirlwind shop in Manhattan…'

'*We…?*'

'I can't say that shopping with a woman is something I ever do, but I'm willing to make an exception...'

'That's very considerate of you, Theo, but I'll manage just fine with what I've brought with me.'

Thank heavens for the two big books. She anticipated doing a *lot* of reading. Although she wouldn't be able to hide away—not when there would be other people around whose mission it was to entertain the newly engaged couple.

'I think I'm going to get some sleep now.' She pointedly turned away and nestled herself into a suitably dormant position, although her mind was still all over the place.

She didn't want to think about it. What was the point?

'Don't wake me for food,' she muttered, turning her head, and Theo, who had already extracted his laptop from his case, grinned at her.

'Are you *sulking*?'

'I don't like plane food.'

'It will be far more relaxing at a house...away from the noise and chaos of the city...'

Alexa didn't bother to answer, because she just *knew* that he was having a laugh at her expense. Instead she snatched the airline blanket and covered herself as much as she could without ducking under it completely.

Relaxing? How much 'relaxing' did a mouse do in a lion's den?

But she was far more tired than she had thought. She had had a sleepless night... The low thrum of the plane's engine, the dimming of the cabin lights...

She fell asleep for the duration of the seven-hour flight and was pleasantly surprised to be shaken awake when the sign flashed on for seat belts to be fastened.

Her mouth was dry, her hair had rebelled against its restraining braid and was a tousled mess, and she knew that her skin would look as rumpled as the rest of her did.

Too bad.

'Somehow,' Theo greeted her as she struggled into an upright position and stifled a yawn, 'we got lost in conversation about our change of plan and I forgot to give you my little present...'

The man looked unfairly bright-eyed and bushy-tailed. Had he worked solidly for the entire flight? Alexa hoped that she hadn't flopped against him accidentally, or snored or dribbled, and she hastily undid her plait and sifted her fingers through her hair in an attempt to get it looking a little less like a bird's nest.

'I'm not sure I can deal with any more surprises,' she told him truthfully.

Her nostrils flared as she breathed in his woody after-shave, and when she glanced down she was momentarily mesmerised by the dark sprinkling of hair on his forearm. She could see the strength of muscle and sinew when he flexed his fingers, and she wondered...

Appalled, she tore her eyes away to find him holding a box out to her. He flipped open the lid and there, nestled in a bed of dark blue velvet, was an engagement ring. Not *the* engagement ring, which was currently being altered, but a smaller version.

Alexa had privately thought the original one was a bit on the gaudy side, but she loved the tiny diamond twinkling up at her from this one.

He didn't give her time to protest. Instead he simply stuck the ring on her finger and then looked at it with satisfaction. 'That will do,' he said, holding her finger between his and examining it.

'What on earth is *this* for?'

'Something to wear until the one you chose at the jeweller's is returned.'

'Why do I have to wear something in the meanwhile?' She furtively looked at her finger. It was weird, but this much smaller, less conspicuous ring actually made her feel more *engaged*.

'Humour me. I'm a traditionalist. I like the world knowing that you're my woman...'

Their eyes tangled and he smiled slowly.

Laughing at her again! Yet Alexa couldn't halt the liquid heat pooling between her legs or the tight pinch of her nipples scraping against her lacy bra. She couldn't ignore the effect that low, husky, amused voice had on her weak, weak body.

Her breath caught in her throat and she turned away quickly, hoping that those shrewd, knowing eyes wouldn't gauge her spontaneous reaction.

Thankfully, the plane was descending. She would focus on that, and on checking her bag—which she hadn't opened at all, so there was absolutely no point in making sure that everything was correct and present. But it was a distraction.

They weren't going to be driven to the Hamptons. Instead they would be whooshed there by helicopter, because Bob had extensive gardens—big enough for several helicopters to land and take off, it would seem.

Theo told her all this as they were whisked through Immigration and on to where they could collect their bags.

'I really was looking forward to going to all the art galleries,' Alexa returned wistfully as they were transported like royalty to where the helicopter was waiting for them.

It was hot and sunny and a perfect day for sightseeing.

'Something can be arranged, I'm sure, if you're really desperate. Felicity would probably love to accompany you. If my memory serves me right, she's into that sort of thing... I shall be preoccupied during the day, at any rate...'

Alexa shuddered at the prospect of trekking down to Manhattan in the company of someone else. Strolling

through art galleries had always been a pleasurable thing
to do on her own—a time for quiet reflection and a bit of
peace and quiet.

'How many people are going to be there?' she asked,
gazing idly around her as the stretch limo removed them
from the main airport,

'A handful.' His phone buzzed and he picked up the call
and remained talking, only cutting short his conversation
when their helicopter was within sight.

'Work,' he said crisply.

'Is that all you ever think about?' Alexa asked, eyeing
the helicopter with trepidation. She had been on a helicopter twice in her life and had hated both experiences.

'Not *all*...'

There was a small, knowing smile on his lips and she
shook her head with exasperation.

'Work and flings, then...'

Theo burst out laughing and made a big show of stepping back and helping her into the helicopter. He exchanged a few pleasantries with their pilot and then turned
to her, the smile still lingering on his lips.

'Don't knock a good fling. Flings can be very
satisfying—as I'm sure you've discovered for yourself,
considering you've never married...'

'I can't see anything satisfying in meaningless sex!'
Alexa had to half shout as the scream of the rotor blades
threatened to drown out conversation.

'I prefer to call it *no strings sex.* And what about *fun*?'
Theo prompted. 'Or is that something you disapprove of?
Along with kicking back?'

'I just think it must get very boring after a while,' she
bristled.

'In which case your "meaningless sex" can't have been
very exciting.'

Alexa ignored that. Did he think that she spent her time

hopping in and out of bed with random men? Hadn't he seen for himself that she wasn't like that? She didn't know whether to be relieved or insulted at his one-track mind, but she did know that it was hardly surprising, because he was simply judging her according to his own standards.

He had no problem disengaging his emotions from the act of sexual intercourse. For him it was no more meaningful than a physical workout at the gym. And his relationships, if they could be called that, probably didn't last much longer.

Thankfully, *she* had never been like that—which was some consolation considering she fancied the man.

At least she knew where her priorities were, and would never allow the physical to take over.

She didn't reply to his provocative statement. Instead she stared down at the wispy clouds and thought that in a week's time all of this would be over—and thank goodness for that.

CHAPTER SEVEN

ALEXA HAD NO time to let panic get a grip because the helicopter ride was over practically before it had begun, and then it was buzzing and lowering itself down to a section of lawn which had been converted into a neat helipad.

She had no idea what to expect, but she did know that if Theo had referred to his friend's house as 'a mansion', then it was going to be pretty spectacular—and it was.

She had seen there was a pool from above—a rectangle of pristine bright blue—but the view of the top of the house didn't do justice to its splendour, which only became apparent as they were transported in something resembling a motorised golf buggy to the curving courtyard.

On either side of the drive immaculate lawns stretched towards hedgerows that had been clipped with razor-sharp precision, high enough to ensure perfect privacy. The house was fronted by a series of striking columns that threw the sprawling veranda at the front into cool shade. On the first floor a similar veranda mimicked the one below, but circled the entire house, providing a massive outdoor deck space on which she could spot clusters of shaded furniture. The top floor was more modest, sheltered by an overhanging terracotta roof, and at the four corners of the house massive chimneys advertised indoor fireplaces.

'Huge...' Alexa was duly impressed, even though she

was accustomed to grand houses. 'How many people live here?'

'Four, once upon a time. Now just two, because both kids have left home. As you might gather, they're not my contemporaries. I met them a long time ago, when my father was involved in lending Bob cash to fund his dream of building a golf and country club. The golf and country club is now one of the most frequented by top professional golfers, and he's dabbled in a series of other successful ventures since those heady days.'

'You must have been very young at the time.'

Theo looked down at her and grinned. 'I challenged Bob to a game of golf and whipped him. Since then we've been firm friends...'

'*That's* something else you do,' she couldn't resist murmuring.

'Come again?'

'By way of relaxing... You play golf.'

'Would you like to know which form of relaxation I prefer?'

'No, I wouldn't!'

'You're so predictable in your responses...'

Suddenly he pulled her towards him and tucked her against his body—and, sure enough, waiting in the open doorway was a small blonde woman in her fifties, her face wreathed with smiles.

'Bob never thought you'd do it, you great big lug! But I *knew* that a woman would come along and sweep you off your feet! I'm Felicity, by the way, and you have to excuse my shrieking like a crazy person but we were just so darned *surprised* when we heard that our favourite boy in the *whole wide world* was finally going to settle down!'

In between speaking at rapid-fire speed and introducing herself Felicity managed to plant a friendly kiss on both their cheeks while hustling them into the house and calling out for 'Stanley' to take their bags up.

Alexa had no time to say any of the usual polite things about the house or about their trip or about anything at all.

'Like it or not, you're gonna tell all! *Bob!* Bob's in the middle of one those darned conference calls!'

This to Alexa, with a woman-to-woman wink.

'You make sure when you've got a ring on this guy's finger that you ban all conference calls! And make sure he doesn't take up golf! I've had to start taking lessons or else lose that lug of a husband of mine to fairways and putting greens!'

No concessions were made to the fact that they had been travelling for several hours. Felicity dragged them through the house at breakneck speed, towards a massive kitchen which was the last word in high-tech. Glossy white built-in cupboards concealed everything, and the gleaming marble countertops were bare of all but the essentials. She led them on towards some comfortable seating in a conservatory that overlooked the manicured lawns, and once they were seated offered tall glasses of homemade lemonade whilst promising them that they could 'go freshen up' just as soon as they'd spilled the beans.

'I've got to grab you two kids before the house becomes a hotbed for dull businessmen!' She settled comfortably into one of the chairs and peered at them with lively curiosity.

Alexa could see fine laughter lines around her eyes and mouth. This was a warm, giving woman who loved to laugh and have fun. That was apparent in the way she spoke and the way she punctuated everything she said with a little breathless laugh.

'So, what does it feel like to be in love?' She directed the question to Theo, but her twinkling eyes darted between both of them. She was obviously delighted at their engagement.

Next to her, Theo still had his arm around her shoulders and it took a lot of effort not to shuffle a few inches away. Now that she had faced up to her inconvenient attraction Alexa was finding it impossible to keep her body's responses under control.

'A refreshing change,' he said.

Alexa kept her smile pinned to her face and tried to wax lyrical when Felicity looked at her for more of a gushy explanation. 'Wonderful!' she chirped. 'We never thought in a million years that...er...when we met we would end up...well...'

'In the throes of heady love? Is that what you were going to say, my darling?'

Felicity needed no more encouragement to launch into an impassioned speech about the wonders of love, after which she quizzed Alexa about her family, about what she did, expressing earnest approval of her volunteer work. Everything was interspersed with smug, smiling nods that said Theo had indeed found the perfect woman.

At that point Bob appeared, and there were more introductions and an excited synopsis of everything that had been said in his absence.

These were Theo's good friends and, looking at their interaction, Alexa could see a side of him that had not been in evidence before. He was warm, thoughtful, interested...and utterly, utterly charming. He had ensured that their daughter in Australia was introduced to a social network, thanks to his brother. He had personally chaperoned their youngest daughter when she had travelled to Europe as a sixteen-year-old, making sure that the family to whom she had been sent on an exchange visit was vetted and ticked all the boxes.

She had a new picture of him, and it wasn't the sarcastic, ruthless guy who provoked her and rubbed her up the wrong way.

'I feel like I've been tossed into a cyclone,' she said, when they finally left their hosts to prepare a barbecue for later.

Theo grinned. 'They like you. And you'll get used to their high-octane energy.'

Ahead of them Stanley, one of the staff, had disappeared along the corridor. The house seemed bigger on the inside than it did on the outside, and it was furnished in a beautifully airy, plantation style. The paintings on the walls were bright and eclectic, and the marble flooring on the ground floor gave way to rich, deep wood on the first floor.

She was so preoccupied with admiring the rooms they passed that she only realised that they had arrived at a bedroom when she noticed Stanley disappearing back towards the stairs, and then, as she entered, she looked around her with mounting panic.

'It's a bedroom,' she said in a high voice.

Theo had strolled towards the window, and now he turned to look at her for a few seconds, before moving to quietly close the door behind them. 'Well observed.'

'I'm not *sharing* a bedroom with you.'

Had it crossed her mind that they would be put in the same room? If it had, then the thought hadn't registered long enough to take root. She had glibly assumed that they would be housed in separate rooms... The place must have dozens of rooms, for heaven's sake!

'That is exactly what you'll be doing,' Theo told her, his voice hard.

He stood in front of her, an implacable rock, until she had no choice but to look up at him.

'Furthermore, you're going to compliment Felicity on the room and tell her how fantastic it is being here instead of in a boring, impersonal hotel in Manhattan. Bob and Felicity have bent over backwards to have us here and you're going to be suitably grateful.'

'I'm not sharing a bed with you,' Alexa said, stubbornly holding her ground.

Just thinking about that made the hairs on her hand stand on end. She could imagine his big, muscular body rolling accidentally against hers in the middle of the night and she cringed. She didn't care whether he fancied her or not. She didn't care that she wasn't his type. She cared about the fact that she would combust if they were in the same bed together.

And furthermore... *Did he even sleep with anything on?* He didn't strike her as the flannel pyjamas type...

Theo eyed the chaise longue by the window. 'Fine. In that case the chaise longue is all yours... I'm way too big for that thing.'

'A gentleman would offer to sleep on the floor,' Alexa gritted through pearly white teeth.

'Considering you've already written me off as not being one of those, it's fair to say that I won't be sleeping on the floor. However, you're more than welcome to make *your* bed down there if you like. Now, I'm going to have a shower.'

For a few seconds Alexa remained staring at him in sheer, angry frustration—until it dawned on her that he was beginning to take his clothes off, at which point every nerve in her body was galvanised into horrified action and she spun round to speak with her back to him.

'Do you mind getting undressed in the bathroom?' she hissed, and she heard his throaty chuckle in response.

'Why? Don't tell me that you've never seen a man's naked body before?'

Alexa seethed. 'I won't even bother to answer that!'

Not only did he continue chuckling, he actually *whistled* as he disappeared into the bathroom, thankfully closing the door behind him and giving her time to unpack her clothes at the speed of light.

He emerged ten minutes later, a towel casually wrapped round his waist.

Alexa, about to reach for her bundle of clothing, was frozen to the spot. Background noises faded and all she could hear was the frantic thud of her heartbeat.

The man was...*spectacular.*

Bronzed, muscled, broad-shouldered. Not an ounce of body fat. He was utterly, utterly perfect and she could feel her skin prickle with heat. It was as if something alien and unfamiliar had invaded every nook and cranny of her body.

'I'm going to have a bath now!' Her voice was high-pitched and she cleared her throat. 'I'll meet you down-stairs.'

'Oh, I think it would far more fitting if we were to head down together. Hand in hand.'

Right now *his* hand was reaching to hook the edge of the towel and she fled, slamming and locking the bath-room door behind her.

She barely noticed the over-the-top luxury of the marble bathroom suite, or the little touches that had been given to make it welcoming. The fragrant pot-pourri, the fluffy white towels, the dinky soaps and shampoos...

She couldn't concentrate on anything but the fact that Theo was in the next room...*probably strolling around in his birthday suit while he decided what to wear...*

She took as long a bath as was humanly possible, and then dressed and applied her make-up in the bathroom, peering into the steamed-up mirror and finally abandon-ing the effort because she could barely make out her re-flection. Her hair she left just as it was, long and tangled, and she finally emerged with only her shoes to put on.

He was sprawled on the bed, half naked, just his trou-sers on, with a book casually propped on his bare stomach. He peered at her over the top of it as she walked into the room.

'How *dare* you go into my bag?'

Theo inspected the book cover and grinned. 'Shall I tell you how it ends or will that spoil the surprise?'

'I thought you might have got dressed!'

'I was about to put my shirt on but this gaudy book jacket grabbed my attention. Of course I figured out who did it by page four, but I thought I'd check to confirm— and, sure enough, I was right.'

He chucked the book and it landed neatly back in her bag, which was on the ground, half open.

'Nice outfit.' Taking his time, he slid his legs over the side of the bed and sauntered towards the wardrobe to extract a shirt. 'The bed's very comfortable. Shame you won't be experiencing it. You'll be trying to find a comfy position on the chaise longue or on the floor...'

'You're... You're...'

'Shall we head down?'

He waited by the door for her, watching as she stepped into some sandals with little wedge heels. He didn't think she realised just how damned sexy she looked in that strappy little sundress, with her long hair tumbling all over the place. Even her scowl couldn't detract from the picture.

Difficult, feisty, mulish and prickly as hell. Who would have thought that *sexy* could come in that package?

He offered his arm and Alexa stormily hooked her hand in the crook as they descended the stairs. He was as cool as the proverbial cucumber, telling her about the history of the house and the antics of the infamous gardener who had landscaped the grounds. Admittedly it was very interesting, and she was big enough to tell him so before Bob and Felicity took over the rest of the evening.

It was relaxed, and they made charming, inquisitive and interesting hosts. Bob had hundreds of amusing anecdotes about the famous golf players he had met over the years…a golf game was arranged…the barbecue was exquisite and informal and champagne flowed. Alexa was even aware that she was laughing at one point as glasses were raised to toast the couple.

But could she relax? Not a bit of it.

Every nerve in her body was stretched to breaking point because all she could think about was that room…that bed…and Theo lying with the duvet half on, half off, possibly clothed but more likely not…

She was spent by the time the evening was at an end. She liked both their hosts, and she could see that they were thrilled at what they considered a wonderful love match. If only they knew!

'So…' Theo flung open the bedroom door and stood aside to let her pass, then shut it behind him and lounged against it, arms folded, a slight smile curving his mouth. 'Did you enjoy the evening?'

The confines of the bedroom and the daunting prospect of the night ahead, not to mention all the other nights ahead, slammed into her with the force of a sledgehammer.

'I…I really did, as a matter of fact,' Alexa replied nervously. She remained standing by the window on the opposite side of the bedroom, with the yawning space of rug-covered floor between them. 'I had no idea what to expect of your friends, but they're incredibly nice and hospitable…'

And that, by association, said something about the man towering in front of her. She relaxed. She had nothing to fear in sharing a bedroom with him. He'd been nothing but decent in accepting her terms and, frankly, putting up with her moods. She'd sniped and argued and fought him every inch of the way when *he* hadn't been the one who had dumped her in this situation. She had used him as a scapegoat for her own frustrations and, arrogant though the man was, he had not retaliated in kind.

'I…er…just want to apologise…'

Theo looked at her in surprise and pushed himself away from the door to kick off his shoes. He began unbuttoning his shirt and Alexa fought to stay calm and hold on to her relaxed frame of mind.

'Apologise for what?'

'I haven't been the easiest person to be around…'

'Really?' Theo said drily. 'I'm glad you brought that to my attention. I wouldn't have noticed otherwise.'

'Not that *you've* been plain sailing!'

Theo burst out laughing and Alexa reluctantly smiled.

'Some men might find your fighting spirit a little challenging, but I admit that I'm growing to rather like it. And now that we've established a fragile truce I wouldn't want to ruin it by forcing you to build your nest on the chaise longue, so I'll take the floor.'

Alexa nodded.

Good.

But it was a super king-sized bed, and the floor was going to be an uncomfortable resting place even for a guy who probably survived on only a couple of hours sleep a night.

She escaped to the bathroom, washed her face and brushed her teeth and changed into her pyjamas. Feverishly she decided that whilst she *could* continue ranting and railing and behaving like a child, she could also just… trust that new side of him she had seen. He wasn't going to make a pass at her just because they happened to be lying on the same mattress, was he? She had been superimposing her own anxieties on to him and it was foolish.

He took the bathroom after her and she pretended not to notice the fact that he was already half naked…that the button to his trousers was undone…that she could see a sliver of his underwear where the trousers dipped down over his lean hips.

In the fifteen minutes during which she heard the whoosh of water and the sounds of him getting ready she tried to get her racing heartbeat under control, and she was burrowed down under the duvet by the time the bathroom door was flung open.

She sneaked a glance and heaved a sigh of relief that he was still in his boxers.

'Well, well, well...' Theo strolled into the room and registered that she was in the bed but that there was no pile of linen on the floor, waiting to be turned into a sleeping area. Instead she had banked some cushions down the middle of the mattress in a neat dividing line.

Alexa flipped over and feigned a yawn of exhaustion. 'It's silly for either of us to sleep on the floor. The bed is huge and there's no reason why we can't share it like two adults.'

'I like your definition of sharing *like two adults...*' He nodded at the military march of cushions along the middle of the bed.

Reluctantly she grinned. 'I thought it might be a good idea to have separated sides.'

'Of course.'

Theo was amused at just how innocent that gesture was. He climbed into bed, his antennae noting the way she shifted ever so slightly away from him. She was clearly awake, but she wasn't reading her book and she certainly wasn't about to engage in conversation. He reached for his laptop, propped it on his lap and casually asked if it would bother her if he worked for a couple of hours. He was even more amused when she didn't answer.

Bother her? It bothered her that he was even *breathing* next to her, far less working.

Her body was rigid. She would never manage to get a

wink of sleep. She knew that. Nor would she be able to toss and turn. If she tossed and turned he would guess that she was awake, plus she would keep *him* up, and then they'd both be awake…in a bed…just the two of them…

Sleep overcame her. It had been a long and tiring day and her exhausted body at last won the battle over her hyperactive mind.

She dreamt that she was skimming over the clouds, looking down. And then, as she looked behind her, over her shoulder, Theo was advancing, getting closer and closer. Part of her wanted desperately to run away, but another, stronger part was holding her fast and *liked* the fact that she couldn't move, that he would get closer and closer, and their bodies would fuse… She would be able to skim her hands over his broad chest and feel the rough surface of muscle and tendon…

The dream was so real that she could almost feel his hands on her, brushing against her thigh and then curving between her legs. She moaned softly.

Her eyes fluttered open and…she wasn't dreaming.

For a few seconds Alexa was completely disorientated. The strategically positioned cushions had hit the floor at some point during the night, and not only had she rolled towards Theo but right now the palm of her hand was flat against his hard chest and he was as awake as she was.

And holding her against him as if it was the most natural thing in the world.

Her limbs felt heavy and lazy and, just like in her dream, whilst a part of her desperately knew that she should pull away, another part of her felt heavy and warm and lazy, utterly incapable of doing anything but revelling in the feel of his equally warm body.

'Shh…' Theo murmured, as if she had spoken.

After lying in complete silence while he had tried to focus on work Alexa had eventually fallen asleep. He had known by the change in the rhythm of her breathing and, oddly enough, having her asleep next to him had made *him* a little jumpy.

He had managed to subdue his disobedient libido when it had reared its head and he had done that by rationalising it out of existence. He was in an unnatural and forced situation—heading down the aisle and not by choice. He was with a woman whose emotionalism was not the kind of thing he sought or appreciated in *any* woman—certainly not in a woman to whom he was to be married. And, physically, since when had he *ever* gone for small, curvy girls? That had always been his brother's domain.

But just knowing that she was next to him in the bed had kept him awake. At one point he had seriously considered slipping out of bed and heading for a cold shower— especially when those cushions had been kicked away and, like a little mouse gravitating towards the source of warmth, she had wriggled closer and closer until she had been touching him.

'You were moaning,' he whispered. 'Having a bad dream? Or a really good one?'

Alexa squeezed her eyes shut and remembered exactly how erotic that dream of hers had been. Heat was still making her want to snap her legs together.

'I'm sorry if I woke you,' she whispered back. 'The cushions…'

'Turns out that soft furnishings don't make very successful fortifications…' He sifted his fingers through her hair. His body was raging, his libido in full surge—a primitive response over which he had no control.

Right now, right here, Theo wanted her in a way he had never wanted any woman in his life before. This wife-to-be he had never asked for and from whom he knew he should keep a safe distance. Because if he slept with her…slept with someone who was looking for a guy who was most certainly *not him*...that single act of passion would make the next year even more impossibly awkward than it was already showing signs of being.

And yet...

'Why did you feel the need to stick a row of cushions between us?'

His hand dipped to the curve of her waist. She wasn't pulling back with a screech of maidenly outrage and more than anything else *that* was a massive turn-on—because it was proof that despite all her protests she wanted him. She didn't *want* to want him...just as *he* didn't want to want *her*...but their bodies were not on the same page as their intellects.

In a life that was formidably controlled this lack of self-control felt good...satisfying...addictive.

How the hell was he going to endure twelve months of wanting her and banking down his desire?

They were both adults, he reasoned. They fancied one another, and he knew from experience that it was a very short journey between fancying a woman and boredom setting in. He had no doubt that if she fancied him it was something she was fighting to ignore, which meant that the same would apply to her. If they slept together they would rid themselves of an inconvenient lust—a bit like taking the right medicine to kill a fever.

'Did you think...?'

His voice was low and soft, and Alexa knew that it was no shock that she was finding it impossible to pull away from him when he was hypnotising her with his deep, dark, sexy drawl.

'Did you think that if it weren't for some scatter cushions you might have found yourself wanting to touch me?'

'No!'

'Liar.' He laughed softly under his breath. 'I've felt the way your body tenses up every time I've touched you and seen the way you slide hot little glances over at me when you don't think I'm watching you... Except I've been watching you a hell of a lot more than you probably thought. In fact a lot more than I ever anticipated...because I'm feeling what you're feeling...'

'I never said...' Her voice was so feeble and unconvincing that she wasn't surprised when he laughed again.

'Sure about that? Because there's a foolproof way of proving whether you're telling little porky-pies...'

He was going to kiss her—and she wasn't going to fight it. Her body was on fire and she wanted him to touch it... she wanted to touch *his*...and she had never wanted to touch any guy like that—hadn't even come close...

She'd never suspected—not for a second—that lust could trample all over her principles and turn them to mush.

She closed her eyes on a sigh, leaned into him, and Theo, trailing the most delicate of caresses along her jawbone, simultaneously slipped his finger under the baggy nightie and beneath her underwear and into her wetness to finger her.

It was shocking and unexpected, and Alexa wriggled away from the touch, reaching down to push his hand away, squirming free, but knowing that she didn't want to create space between them—she wanted to abolish it.

She shouldn't want this but she did. She *wanted* his fingers exploring her and she burned with mortification. When he slid his hand along her stomach desire held her fast, stopped her from breaking their connection. It felt like an extension of her dream, weird and surreal and somehow *not really happening*—at least not in a way that felt dangerous or threatening.

Her breathing quickened. She heard herself pant a desperate *'No!'* but it felt so good. She slid her treacherous, trembling hands over his chest, yanked them away, repeated the caress, this time tracing the broad, muscled width of his shoulders.

The sexless nightie felt itchy and uncomfortable, and she wanted to squirm out of her underwear—and was immediately horrified and panicked by the impulse.

So she fancied him. And he, to her amazement, fancied *her*. Maybe it was the strangeness of the situation into which they had both been thrown. In fact that was probably it—because if she had bumped into him under normal circumstances, at one of those social events which *she* hated and which *he* saw as part and parcel of being who he was, then she was sure that she would never, ever, have been attracted to him. And he would have had one of those leggy, supermodel airhead types clinging to him like ivy. He wouldn't have given *her* a second glance.

But here they were...

She tentatively let her hand stray to his waist, and then a bit lower, and she shivered as she felt the massive bulge of his erection pushing against the boxers. It was terrifying, and she withdrew her hand as though she'd suddenly plunged it into an open fire.

But she wanted to touch him *so badly...*

'Theo...this is crazy...'

'Is it? I don't think so. In the whole crazy charade, this feels like the least crazy bit...'

'I don't do this sort of thing.'

'You mean make love to your fiancé?'

'You know what I mean.'

'I know what you mean, my dearest wife-to-be. But do you *want* to...?'

'Yes! No... Oh, I don't know... Theo! I can't think straight...not when you're touching me...'

'Not thinking straight suits me—and what does "Yes! No... I don't know..." mean?'

'It means I find you attractive. Okay?'

'Okay.'

He'd never had to ask a woman if she wanted him, had never received such a grudging response, but hearing her say that put him on top of the world.

He gradually pushed up the nightie. He was as out of control as a horny teenager about to lose his virginity. *Crazy.* He cupped the fullness of her breast and then rubbed his thumb over her stiff nipple, over and over, until she was moaning and moving restlessly against him.

'We shouldn't…' In the grip of the sensations that were bombarding her on all fronts she could barely get the pathetically weak protest out.

'Life is too short for *shouldn't…*'

'That's easy for you to say.'

You're experienced. You haven't spent your life welding sex to love and waiting for them to come along at the same time. You're relaxed and carefree about this sort of thing. Not like me.

And yet for all that she couldn't have shifted out of his reach if she'd tried.

'You've done nothing but fight me,' he moaned softly. 'Now I want you to tell me that you need this as much as I do…'

'I…'

'*Say it*, Alexa…'

'I want this so much,' she confessed shakily, thrilled at the hot urgency in his voice.

'Good.' His voice was thick with satisfaction.

He lowered his head, angling her body so that he could lick and kiss her neck, her shoulders. He nearly lost it completely when he felt the hitch in her breathing as he trailed kisses over her breasts, until finally he clamped his mouth over the big, pink circular disc of her nipple.

Her whole body tensed, and then relaxed into the caress. He was dimly aware of the fluttering of her fingers in his hair as he continued to draw the stiffened bud of her throbbing nipple deep into his mouth, nipping and suckling on it. He was a big man, with big hands, and the abundance of her breasts was a good fit as he cupped her other breast and massaged it.

'Touch me,' he commanded roughly, pulling her hand down and clasping it hard over his erection. 'Just hold me. *Tight*, for God's sake. I don't want to spoil the party prematurely...'

He reared up as she obeyed and took a few deep breaths, fighting to recover some of his lost self-control. When his breathing finally levelled out he resumed where he had left off, this time devoting his attention to her other breast, but not until he had looked at her nakedness, feasting his eyes on the paleness of her skin and the contrasting rosy flush of her nipples.

Alexa gazed up at him through half-closed eyes. He had rid himself of his boxers and his erection was a thick, hard, pulsing rod of steel. There wasn't a shred of self-consciousness in him as he watched her gazing at him. She was scared, thrilled, massively turned on...all at the same time.

'Would you like to sample the fare...?' He asked, and when she frowned in bewilderment he grinned. 'Taste with your mouth what you're busy tasting with your eyes...?'

He couldn't understand her... She was enthusiastic, turned on, and yet curiously shy and hesitant. But, then again, the women he slept with were all so experienced that perhaps he had forgotten what it was like to be with one who didn't see sex as an exercise in impressing him with gymnastics. He liked it. He knew that.

'I... I'm not... I don't... This is all so far out of my comfort zone...'

'Then I'll let you set the pace...'

He was moved by the nervousness in her voice. She

wanted him, but she wasn't going to jump on him, and he got that. She needed to be treated like a delicate piece of porcelain china. He needed to let her have control. And that turned him on.

She covered him with tentative little kisses. She clearly liked him to touch her breasts and he did. But he wanted her to hold his erection, and after a while, after she had trailed delicate little kisses over his stomach—kisses that were driving him mad, had she but known it—she garnered the courage to take those delicate little kisses lower down.

She whimpered softly, and those little whimpers were a turn-on beyond belief. To a man with a fairly jaded palette when it came to the opposite sex and their bedroom antics, this was uniquely refreshing. She was shy. He wanted her to feel comfortable with his body, comfortable to touch him wherever she wanted, but the way she took her time... *agony*. He could barely breathe.

To Alexa, witnessing this big, utterly confident and controlled man lose it a little was as heady as a dose of adrenaline shot straight into her system.

Her faltering self-confidence strengthened into a growing sense of liberation. A guy who was restless and impatient, who took what he wanted whatever the cost—a guy for whom *tomorrow* was not a word in his vocabulary if it could be replaced by *today*—was letting her take charge, and that felt so good to her.

She straightened and looked down at him. She'd never been naked in front of a man in her life before, and her skin tingled and burned as he gazed at her with open, unashamed desire.

When he reached forward to graze his thumbs across her stiff nipples she moaned softly and closed her eyes. Her whole body was trembling.

She wanted more than this. She wanted him inside her, moving inside her, filling her up...

She guided his hand between her legs and even as she did so was shocked at her forwardness. When he began massaging her there she covered his hand with hers, groaned as he slid two fingers inside, unerringly finding her clitoris and sending her into spiralling, ever-increasing zones of sexual pleasure.

She felt like a rag doll. As her pleasure grew...and grew... and grew...she opened dazed eyes and levelled them at him.

'I want more, Theo.' She barely recognised her own voice, which was husky with desire.

'And so do I... You have no idea... But...' He reached for his wallet on the dressing table to extract a condom. 'Life right now,' he murmured, catching her heated gaze and holding it, 'is complicated enough without adding to it...'

CHAPTER EIGHT

HE DROPPED THE condom on the side table and settled over her, grazing between her legs with his erection, nudging, but not too much. And then he slid his hands under her back, arching her up towards him. Nerves mingled with wicked anticipation, and anticipation won.

She had disposed of her nightie—flung it over the side of the bed. She knew that she should be feeling timid, quailing at his frank inspection of her body, but there was open heat in his lazy gaze. No mistaking the fact that he was hot for her. She didn't think that his heat could match her own.

'I'm fat…' she confessed, burning up like straw flung to a struck match.

'Whoever told you that? Surely not your parents…?'

He didn't normally do pillow talk, but the openness of her admission touched him. He lay down next to her and pulled her against him. He could feel the steady beating of her heart and the squash of her breasts against his chest.

A slight delay to proceedings. There was nothing un-cool about that. In fact it made sense, gave his body time to adjust to its normal tempo.

'Gosh, no.'

This intimacy felt good. Not so much sex for the sake of sex as two people in bed about to make love. She had a gut feeling that he wasn't the kind of guy who slowed down to accommodate anyone, and that included the women he took to his bed. But he was slowing down for *her*. And whilst the logical part of her knew that it meant nothing, it still felt good.

Plus… Rushing into sex…

Yes, her body was on fire for him, but her mind was tentative, filled with her own shortcomings and what he might say about them. If he'd made some great big show of trying to get her into bed she might have stood a chance at resistance, but like this…in the dead of night…here in this bed…she was powerless to fight her body's urgings.

Talking like this might relax her…

'The opposite.' She traced the outline of his shoulders, liking its tough ridges and contours. 'My parents always told me that I was beautiful and that I could do anything I wanted.' She laughed a little breathlessly, because confiding wasn't something she was accustomed to doing. She marvelled that she was doing it now, with this man. 'Of course most parents say that, and I wasn't a complete idiot. I knew I wasn't beautiful.'

'And you knew that because…? You had a magic mirror on your wall…?'

Alexa laughed, but there was a telling catch in her laughter and Theo experienced a moment of disorientation during which he felt weirdly tender and possessive towards this prickly, argumentative woman who had given him nothing but a hard time ever since their paths had crossed.

'I overheard a conversation when I was eleven,' she confessed. 'I was in a toilet cubicle at school and I overheard some of my friends giggling about me. I'd never thought I was fat but it seems that I was…and I had also developed way ahead of everyone else. That's a big deal when you're a kid. Whilst all the girls in my year were busy shooting up like beanpoles I was getting…well…*a figure…* It seems I was something of a figure of fun…especially to boys…'

'Boys that age can be idiots,' Theo told her fiercely. He dropped a kiss on her forehead and held her against him, her face pressed against his neck. 'In fact...' he angled her so that he could look down at her seriously '...quite a few idiot boys grow up into idiot men.'

Was that her opinion of him? A guy who judged by appearances only?

He sensed that that was just the sort of introspective question that might not benefit from too much in-depth analysis. Her whole persona now made sense to him. Her defensiveness...her passionate interest in the intellectual as opposed to the physical...her mulish aversion to the sort of high society affairs where she might feel herself judged, yet again, on appearance instead of personality.

The fact that she was here now, playing at a relationship with the sort of man she had probably spent her entire adult life erecting walls to keep out, spoke volumes about her close relationship with her parents.

'I suppose...' She laughed a little self-consciously. 'Thanks for listening...'

Theo was highly offended. 'Of course I listened to you! Why wouldn't I?'

'Because you don't listen a lot when women moan and whine?' she suggested teasingly.

Theo had the grace to flush. 'Maybe that whining and moaning always had a certain predictable flavour...'

'What do you mean?'

'We're having a conversation,' Theo heard himself say.

Alexa nestled against him, nerves temporarily banished. 'Isn't that what you told me we *had* to do, considering we're about to tie the knot?'

'I don't do a lot of that either,' he admitted with a wry smile.

'Talking in bed with a woman?'

Theo thought that it might have been more accurate to

say *talking*, and leave it at that, but of course he *did* talk to women… Regrettably, the conversations were not usually of an inspiring nature and, having never—not once—thought about that, he now wondered whether he had set his standards a little on the low side in the past. At least insofar as intellectual stimulation was concerned.

'There always seem to be far more exciting things to do than chit-chat…' He shoved aside the niggling moment of introspection and returned to the business of making love—his comfort zone.

He curved his hand along her side, smoothing it over her rounded hip and confidently inserting it between her legs, parting them and laughing under his breath at her little pant of anticipation.

This was *definitely* more like it.

'Now it's time for you to lie back and think of England…'

'Is that an order?'

'Of course it is. Haven't we already established that I'm the arrogant sort, who gives orders and expects them to be obeyed…?'

Alexa giggled breathlessly and closed her eyes—although she knew the last thing she would be doing was thinking of England…

He explored her body and took his time doing it, suckling on her swollen nipples, arching her body up so that he could enjoy them all the more. The longer he spent there, the more she frantically wanted him to go further, and her whole body was tingling as he made his way down, inch by inch, until his mouth found the dampness between his legs.

Alexa gave a little yelp and tried to wriggle away, but Theo pinned her down by her hips and glanced up at her.

'What's the problem?'

'There's something you should know…'

She had debated whether to say anything or not. Could

a man tell the difference between a virgin and a woman who was not? Alexa didn't know, but she knew that she would reveal the full extent of her inexperience the very second he started getting too intimate.

As he had just been doing.

'Hasn't anyone been intimate with you like that?' Theo was tickled pink by that. 'Shh... Time for me to show you what you've been missing...'

He didn't want her to think about this. He just wanted her to *enjoy*. He gently parted her legs and felt her tense. He licked the inside of her thigh and she relaxed with a soft moan, and then, so slowly, he began to explore her.

She tasted of musk and honey, fragrant and seductive. He licked her, and then darted his questing tongue, touching the protruding nub of her clitoris. After gently smoothing her thighs he parted the lips concealing her womanhood with his fingers, so that her sensitive clitoris was even more exposed to the erotic dance of his tongue.

Alexa groaned. She could barely breathe, the pleasure was so intense.

She shielded her face with her arm and twisted away. She was so wet down there...melting like candle wax.

The pleasure became more and more intense, spiralling until she was hurtling towards the edge, and only then did Theo slowly ease his rhythm, leaving her begging for more, pleading with him to bring her to orgasm.

By which time he was so shockingly turned on that he could barely steady his hands to apply the condom. More than anything else, he wanted to come inside her, to feel her wet tightness wrap around his erection...

Alexa stayed him with one trembling hand and gulped. 'There's something I should tell you...'

'Alexa... Not now... I want you so much I'm not sure I'm going to be able to withstand another conversation—

not unless we pause for an intermission and I have a cold shower...'

'It's...it's something you really need to know, Theo,' she said with wrenching urgency.

Theo stilled and gazed down at her flushed cheeks. He couldn't imagine what she might have to say that couldn't keep. She was as turned on as he was and he could barely think straight. Add to that the fact that he was highly experienced and you didn't need to join too many dots to work out how explosive her effect on him was.

Was she about to tell him that she was involved with someone else? It was a question he had asked of her before and she had given a negative response—but that might have been a diplomatic denial, intended to halt a sticky conversation.

With a jolt of surprise he realised that he had already formed assumptions about her, and one of them was that he believed she was genuine—and that annoyed him, because he was cynical when it came to members of the opposite sex.

'If you're going to break my heart by telling me you've got the hots for another man, then it's a conversation I have no interest in having.'

He lay back and felt her nestle against him, propping herself up against his chest. Her long hair hung on either side of her heart-shaped face, a jumble of curls.

'What are you talking about?' Alexa was genuinely puzzled. 'If I had the hots for someone else why would I be...? Well...'

Theo dealt her a slashing grin, relieved at the earnestness in her voice. He curled his fingers into her hair and tugged her down to kiss him.

'Then what...?' he murmured huskily. 'Spill the beans...'

'I've... I'm probably not as experienced as you think I am...'

'What are you telling me?'

'I've never...never done this before...' Alexa said bluntly, holding her breath for his appalled reaction.

'You're a *virgin*?'

'And you're shocked.' She miserably filled in the blanks.

Shocked? No. Surprised? Yes. In his experience virgins in their twenties were about as common as sightings of the dodo. But he was also massively turned on at her admission.

He flipped her over so that he was looking down at her. *His woman.* He should have been turned off, but he wasn't. The opposite.

'I'll take my time,' he murmured. 'And by the time I'm ready to enter you, Alexa, you'll be so wet and ready for me...'

Words failed him.

Who needed words? He was going to give her an experience that would live with her for ever.

He explored her body all over again. He nuzzled and licked her nipples until they were warm and throbbing in his mouth. He trailed languorous kisses along her stomach and as he did so slowly rubbed her clitoris with his fingers, readying her for his mouth.

Alexa raised her legs, squirming as he nuzzled between her legs. Just watching his dark head there was the most erotic thing she could ever have imagined. True to his word, he took his time, and she knew, inexperienced as she was, that it would require a lot of willpower for him to do so.

'I don't want to...to come like this...' she gasped, as her body began sweeping her towards the edge.

Theo looked up from where he had been busy and shot her a lazy smile. 'You won't...'

He'd also promised to be gentle, and he was. He nudged his way into her and she felt herself open up for him, and when he began to thrust into her she was crying out for him, her hands curling into his hair, her body arching up so that he could take her completely. Any fleeting discomfort was quickly overwhelmed by a surge of *want* and she came with soaring intensity. It was an out-of-body experience that left her shaking.

She didn't want to let him go. She wanted to cling, to feel his perspiring body pressed up against her. She felt him as he came, shuddering inside her on a broken groan of satisfaction. There were no barriers between them in that moment of total surrender and she wished that she could hang on to the moment for ever.

When he reared up to discard the condom, she *missed* him.

'Did the earth move for you?' Theo teased, settling down next to her and pulling her into position so that they were both on their sides, bodies pressed close together. He could have done it all again, but he would have to exercise restraint even though her nakedness was continuing to drive him crazy.

Alexa lowered her eyes, because the feeling of sudden tenderness confused her. He'd stopped being a cardboard cut-out, and that was worrying, but she felt helpless to do anything about it. She couldn't seem to recover her anger at the situation she was in.

'So, no men before me?' Theo mused. 'Tell me why...'

Alexa shrugged.

'You're not going to get away with that. Didn't you have boyfriends at university?'

'Honestly...?' she mused pensively. 'Like I said, I wasn't all that confident about the way I looked. I have an old-fashioned figure...'

'Hourglass. It's a shape that never goes out of style.'

Alexa laughed, liking the compliment even if it wasn't true. 'I guess I watched what my peer group was getting up to from the age of fifteen and knew that I couldn't compete, so I decided I was just going to find my own path and that was academic. I really threw myself into my degree. Yes, of course I went out—but in a group. I'd already decided that I would only give myself to someone if I was in a loving relationship that was going somewhere...'

With dismay, she heard just how that sounded and was quick to rescue him from any false misconceptions. Marriage or not, he wasn't in this out of any genuine feelings for her and she knew that. It was the same for her!

'I didn't think that I could be physically attracted to a man unless I had deeper feelings for him,' she admitted.

'Are you telling me you don't have deeper feelings for me?' Theo drawled, amused. 'Tut-tut... Any self-respecting husband-to-be might be offended by that! Don't underestimate the power of attraction, Alexa. You'd be surprised how many good intentions get trampled on when two free and consenting adults find that they can't keep their hands off one another...and *I* find that I can't keep my hands off *you*. In fact I'd quite like to take you again. Right now. But I won't. I'm a big man, and you'll be sore down there...'

'Theo!'

She traced the outline of his shoulder blade with her finger. *What happens now?* she wanted to ask, but when she thought about that she knew what would happen... They'd have a lavish engagement party, they'd get married and then they'd get divorced. Why did it seem so muddled when it was actually so straightforward?

'I think we need a little time alone to get this out of our systems...' Theo broke through her soul-searching silence.

'What do you mean?'

'Neither of us signed up for this,' he told her matter-of-factly. 'And I'm not just talking about the arranged marriage scenario. *That* particular bombshell was definitely not on the radar for either of us.' He lay back and stared up at the ceiling. 'Neither of us expected that this attraction would jump out at us, did we? But it has, and it's something we have to deal with.'

'Yes...' Alexa parroted faintly, brow furrowed.

Saying that they would *deal* with it somehow removed the element of emotion—turned an unfortunate situation that had taken them by surprise into one that had a solution. He was right. She knew that. But she couldn't stifle the sudden hollowness that settled in the pit of her stomach.

Theo had paused. *A virgin.* She had just discovered that unbridled lust had an unstoppable momentum of its own but he wasn't a fool. She was an incurable romantic and she had lost her virginity to *him*. And he was destined to marry her. The last thing he needed was for her to get in too deep with him.

He fancied her, but he was all wrong for her—in the same way that *she* was all wrong for him. He could never give her what she wanted. He could never give *any* woman the sort of love that took away the ability to think clearly and behave logically. He just didn't have it in him.

He didn't *do* emotions. He played hard, but he always played with his head. She deserved someone who was willing to give her what she wanted. That man wasn't him, and unless they established some ground rules a year might prove a very long time indeed. For both of them.

Being married to someone who might end up expecting more than he was prepared to give would be a recipe for disaster.

'We get this out of our system,' he said flatly, 'and I see no reason why we won't have a harmonious year together.'

'Get it "out of our system"?'

'We can't fight this. We will be in one another's company all the time...'

'What if we weren't?'

'Then it would run its natural course. Lust fades as fast as it comes. That's always been my experience.'

'And you just walk away when that happens?'

'I'm not looking for deep emotional connections, Alexa,' he told her gently. 'For me, a permanent partner will be someone who is prepared to accept that my work will always come first.' He sighed.

'A marriage of convenience with someone who is emotionally switched off...?'

'I wouldn't necessarily describe it like that...'

'Would you fancy her, or would that not matter?'

'We're veering off topic, here.'

'I hear your warning.'

Her drowsy contentment was fading fast. She knew what he was telling her, but just in case she missed the message he was making sure he spelt it out in words of one syllable. *Don't confuse lust with love.* He could give her lust, but love wasn't on the table, and he was probably horrified at the possibility that he might be stuck with someone who'd fall for him.

He was telling her that his boredom threshold would be reached quickly, and that once that happened they would settle into playing the game they were destined to play, with no nasty surprises along the way.

Like unnecessary emotion.

She knew exactly what she should tell *him*. That this had been a one-off. One of those curiosity things... Something that she had succumbed to but which she did not want to repeat.

She opened her mouth and he smoothed his hand over her, between her thighs, and her body suddenly had other things in mind.

'But...' he said.

'But what?' She tried to inject some defiance into her

voice but she heard the way she sounded—helpless and breathy.

'We have options.'

'What are you talking about?'

He had found the damp patch between her legs and was stroking her, finding her sensitive nub and playing with it so that she couldn't think straight.

'You can either retreat back into fighting with me and put this down as a one-night stand...'

Alexa flushed, because that had been her first thought. She had foolishly betrayed all her principles but maybe she could persuade herself that she had put the lapse behind her—because you didn't have to keep repeating a mistake just because you'd made it once.

But how easy was *that* going to be when he could do this to her?

'I can't...can't think...when you're...'

'Let me do the thinking for you.'

'You're so incredibly bossy. Do you *always* have to take charge?'

'Taking charge suits me. I happen to do it very well.'

But this wasn't a decision he wanted her to make on the back of her arousal—even though watching the dazed heat in her eyes and the hectic flush in her cheeks was immensely satisfying. He reluctantly withdrew his hand and rested it in the curve of her waist.

'You'd like to write this off and pretend in the morning that nothing really happened.'

'You can't say that—'

'I can, because I know the way you think, Alexa. You had a fairy-tale dream wedding and a dream guy all mapped out in your head, but instead here we are...'

It irritated him just to voice that, because playing second fiddle to any man—even a fictitious one—just wasn't his thing, but there was no avoiding the truth.

'You know what those marriage vows say...' he drawled, carefully averting his eyes from the tempting glimpse of one pouting pink nipple peeping at him. 'For better or for worse. Loosely interpreting them, I say we should focus on the better side of things for the moment... We fancy each other, incredible though that might be...'

'Thanks very much, Theo.'

'You'd be the first to agree,' he returned wryly. 'You were *horrified* to find out that you would be walking up the aisle with me.'

Alexa didn't want to turn that flat statement back to him—didn't want to hear that he had likewise been horrified to find himself saddled with an emotional and inexperienced girl who—horror of horrors—didn't even have the decency to look like all his supermodel clones.

Truth hurt, and she had faced too many awkward truths recently—not least being this...her attraction to him.

'I would have been horrified to find myself walking up the aisle with *anyone* who wasn't of my own choosing.'

Theo shrugged, because one way or the other it didn't matter.

'I think that instead of denying what's between us we exhaust it—after which the duration of our time together should be as plain sailing as it can be, given the circumstances.'

'We *exhaust* it...?'

'Correct.'

'And do you have a timeline on that?'

If he got bored with all his beautiful conquests after a couple of months, then she gave herself a couple of *weeks.* Oddly, something inside her twisted.

'I prefer to play things by ear—and that cuts both ways. *You* could be the one who gets tired of me...'

Alexa wasn't dim enough to think that he seriously believed that for a minute, but she nodded in agreement.

This wasn't her at all, but he had cut through all the red tape and produced the bald truth of the matter, shorn of all emotion. They carried on having sex until that side of things dwindled away, at which point they would be able to function in one another's company without that sizzle of electricity—which was something he seemed able to handle but which she had found she just couldn't.

She couldn't imagine ever being around him without the hairs on the back of her neck standing on end and her imagination shaking its reins and running wild. It would be like spending a year doing a high wire act without a safety net. Just thinking about it exhausted her.

He was presenting her with a choice. And why not? She couldn't see herself wanting a man indefinitely when he basically wasn't her type anyway. It *would* fizzle out. Of course it would. In the crazy, surreal world into which she had been catapulted it was the one thing that made sense.

And also...

She would be able to give herself permission to enjoy him.

She felt a guilty rush of pleasure at the thought of that.

'I suppose it makes a weird kind of sense...'

She drew that sentence out and filled it with lots of doubt and uncertainty. She didn't want him to feel that she was a push-over simply because she was inexperienced, or that she had become a member of his worshipful fan club. She wanted—*needed* him to think that it was an arrangement that suited her as much as it suited him...that he was as much a virus in her system which she wanted to dispel as she was in his.

'I suppose we can't help the people we're attracted to—even though I always thought I could. I've been edgy around you...and not just because of the circumstances that threw us together. I haven't *liked* being attracted to you, but I'm honest enough to admit that I am. Stupid, and—as you say—passing.'

Theo wasn't sure he liked the word *stupid*, but he wasn't going to get hung up on detail.

Frankly, the faster it passed, the better for him. She was unreasonably distracting and he didn't like distraction—at least not a distraction that seemed to attack without warning and at any given time.

'I have my guys coming tomorrow,' he said. 'My original plan involved a prolonged stay here, with work taking a bit of a back seat to relaxation. This...change in circumstances...requires a change of plan...'

He accompanied that with a slow, curling smile that reminded her just how dangerous a temptation he could be, so thank heavens it wasn't going to be long-lasting.

'How do you mean?'

'We'll just stay for the day. I'll get my business done and then we'll head to Manhattan—finish our stay there. And no adjoining rooms in a penthouse suite...' He stroked the pink, peeping nipple and the little bud hardened under the abrasive rub of his thumb.

'We can't!' Alexa gasped, responding on cue, pulses racing, her whole body slowly heating up once again and then going into meltdown as he continued to rub her nipple.

'Why not?'

'Because it's *rude*! Your friends...they'll be disappointed...'

'They'll be the first to understand. They think this is a love match and they've been trying to brainwash me into the joys of married life for far too long... They'll be over the moon when I tell them that we have to escape for some private time because we can't get enough of one another... I can already hear the violins in the background...'

Little will they expect that this is just a pretend game, and that this so-called need for private time will just be about sex, Alexa thought, with the sort of cynicism she'd never thought she had.

'And your brother's making a big effort to come over... I was quite looking forward to meeting him, maybe going to one of the local art galleries while you were busy during the day...'

Theo burst out laughing. 'Daniel and art *don't* go hand in hand. I think it stems from the fact that an art teacher once told him when he was a kid that he would be doing the world of art a service by staying as far away from pencils and paintbrushes as he could...'

'Whereas you...?'

'*I* was smart enough to work out that if I couldn't paint anything remotely realistic then I'd paint whatever the hell I wanted and call it abstract... It worked... I'll message my brother—tell him to skip the meet-and-greet detour and head directly to the cruise ship he wants to buy...'

'So we go to New York,' Alexa said slowly, 'spend a week there...after which we should both be over this... this...situation between us. Then we return to Italy as a happy, platonic couple and serve our one year's penance before walking away from one another...' She forced a bright smile to her face. 'You're right, of course. Enjoy one another for a few days...get this inconvenient attraction out of our system...and once that little hiccup's dealt with we'll be able to...to look at one another without any stupid awkwardness...'

Since that was pretty much what Theo had had in mind, he was a little unnerved to hear it stated so bluntly.

'Enough talking...' He tilted her head and when she arched back kissed her neck, worked his way to her breasts and then levered himself up and stared down at her flushed face. 'Now I'm going to give you a little lesson on taking charge...'

He did.

She touched him as he had touched her. She straddled him and worked her way meticulously down his body, loving every inch of muscle and sinew under her exploring hands. She marvelled that her shyness had evaporated. Something about the way he looked at her, with a sort of lazy, lingering, heated intensity, stripped her of her inhibitions and invested her with self-confidence she'd never known she possessed.

When she took him in her mouth and heard his throaty groan a heady sense of power invaded her.

There had been moments in her adult life when she had thought about her virginity. She had never been bothered by it, but there had been a nagging worry that when the time came she would be so nervous that she wouldn't be able to enjoy the experience. Sex would have become a big thing she had built up and would fail to deliver on the night.

The only consolation in that scenario had been the certain knowledge that the guy she fell in love with would be someone kind, thoughtful and patient enough to guide her slowly.

As she felt this big, arrogant, sinfully good-looking man shudder as she continued to caress his erect sheath with her mouth and her tongue a thought flew through her head, as lightning-fast as quicksilver...

He might not be a shining advertisement for kind, thoughtful or patient, but he has been kind and thoughtful and patient with me...

The roughened feel of his thighs under her fingers as she continued to arouse him with her mouth took her own physical response to a level she could barely control, and she drew back from her lingering exploration so that she could rub herself against his erection.

Theo was having to take long, even breaths to keep his control in place. He opened his eyes and inhaled sharply as he looked at her astride him.

With one hand firmly on his erection, she flung her head back as she moved her body sensuously against him. Every shudder of pleasure was reflected in her soft moans as his hardness played against her clitoris.

Her long hair was in utter, sexy disarray and her generous breasts bounced as she moved like ripe fruit, gently shaking, too succulent to pass up.

He tugged her towards him so that those breasts were closer to his mouth, and as she knelt over him, still enjoying his erection against her, eyes still shut, breathing still coming and going in little gasps and groans, he flicked his tongue over one engorged nipple and then stilled her slightly so that he could suckle more thoroughly on it.

Hands on her slender ribcage, he carried on pleasuring himself at her breasts until neither of them could handle the build-up any longer.

They were so hot for one another—but she was still cool enough to fumble through his wallet and extract his last condom, which she took her time stretching over him.

Theo was riveted in a way he had never been with any woman by the sight of her voluptuous nakedness...the satiny smoothness of her shoulders and the soft paleness of her skin in such contrast to the perfect circular deep rose of her nipples.

His feeling of absolute possession was second to none, but he easily explained that away by the fact that she had come to him a virgin.

He was going to enjoy being her teacher, and she was showing all the signs of being an A class student...

Who knows? he thought, before his mind emptied of all thought and the primitive responses of his body took over. *Maybe a week might not be quite long enough after all...*

CHAPTER NINE

LYING ON THE BED, Alexa drowsily watched Theo, sitting at the desk in the hotel bedroom, wearing only his boxers, frowning at whatever he was looking at on his computer.

Their last night in Manhattan.

She couldn't quite believe how fast the time had flown since they had left The Hamptons. As predicted, Bob and Felicity had not been at all fazed at their early departure.

'Completely understand!' Felicity had carolled. 'It's been a while—hasn't it, Bobby?—but I can still remember what it was like to be young and in love…!'

Alexa had had to inwardly admit that she and Theo were certainly giving the impression of two people who couldn't keep their hands off one another, and she could understand how that might have led to the misconception that they were in love.

How ironic that now, when there were no reporters around, furiously snapping pictures, the physical contact between herself and Theo was one hundred per cent genuine.

Every time she glanced at him her imagination took over, and she remembered what it felt like to have those hands all over her body and his mouth kissing every enthusiastic inch of her.

They had checked into the penthouse suite which had originally been booked for them—the adjoining room was now redundant—but, frankly, they could have been anywhere in the world. Any hotel in the world. Just so long as there was a bed, because they spent an inordinate amount of time making love.

For a couple of hours every day Alexa had insisted on going out on her own, so that Theo could work.

'I can work perfectly well with you around,' he had drawled, in the sort of dark, persuasive voice that had made her almost but not quite revise her determination not to submerge herself entirely in him. 'In fact I find I work better, because I can touch you whenever I need a break...'

This was just the sort of heady flattery that she knew could so easily go to her head. It was the stuff she loved hearing—just as she loved hearing him tell her how desirable she was, how irresistible, how he couldn't see the bed without wanting her in it, naked and pressed up close to him.

But flattery was all it was, and Alexa knew that she had to steer clear of reading anything else behind it. Because she was getting seriously hooked on touching him, on hearing all those softly murmured words that did wonders for her self-confidence, making her feel utterly desirable...the most desirable woman on the planet.

He'd swept into her life, bringing with him all his worldly experience, and he had used that worldly experience and his unimaginable charm to captivate her.

He had found fertile ground in her, because nothing in her past had prepared her for the impact of their involvement. Had she had *some* experience with the opposite sex she might have had sufficient ammunition to see his charm for what it was...practised, well-used...the same charm that had turned all those other women's heads...

But she'd lacked the necessary experience. And now...

He was completely oblivious to the fact that she was staring at him. It was still only six fifteen in the morning, but she would have bet that he'd been up for at least an hour—maybe more. He seemed to need very little sleep to function.

She gazed at the way his dark hair curled at the nape of his neck, at the muscled width of his shoulders and the tiny mole on his right shoulder, which she could just about make out in the pool of light from the desk lamp he had switched on. He hadn't yet shaved and there was a definite shadow along his jawline. He was frowning, and she knew that in a second he would gently tap his fountain pen on the desk—a habit he had when he was utterly focused on something.

She had asked him why he had a fountain pen when all his work was done on the computer, and he had twirled it in his fingers and told her that it had been a present from his mother when he was eleven. It was his talisman.

There were so many things she felt she now knew about him, and there were so many physical details she had absorbed too, lodging them in her brain the way information was stored on a computer, lying there, ready to be accessed at the flick of a button.

She could recognise the sound of his soft breathing when he was in deep sleep...could tell from the clipped tone of his voice on the phone when he was talking to someone he wanted to get rid of as fast as possible. She had watched him shave in front of the mirror and had come to realise that, although he must surely know just how good-looking he was, he did very little to enhance his looks. No manly moisturisers. He barely looked in a mirror at all.

Her heart began a steady, anxious thud in her chest.

When exactly had she stopped seeing him as the enemy she was shackled to and started seeing him as someone who was witty, beyond intelligent, wickedly charming...?

She knew when she had owned up to her guilty fascination—when she had acknowledged the chemistry between them. But when, exactly, had that undeniable chemistry turned into something deeper for her?

They had strolled through Manhattan, gone to the famous Museum of Modern Art, walked along the High Line and visited the gallery district. She had forgotten that this wasn't a real-life courtship. She had forgotten that those piercing, lazy eyes that roved over her body with rampant appreciation had no intention of lingering there indefinitely.

What had started out for both of them as a perfectly reasonable way of dealing with the inconvenient attraction between them had morphed into something else—*for her.*

She had...

The steady, nervous thud of her heart picked up pace as the enormity and horror of her realisation hit her with the force of a runaway train.

When had she fallen in love with him?

'You're up. Why are you up?'

His dark drawl made her jump, because she had been so busy being dismayed and horrified at her thoughts that she had blanked him out of her line of vision. Now she sat up and feigned a yawn.

'The light must have woken me...' She burrowed back down into the duvet, so that she could take up where she had left off and carry on chewing over her plight—which couldn't have been worse as far as she was concerned.

'In that case I'll switch it off...'

Theo stood up and stretched, and then headed back to the bed—which was just where, for once, Alexa *didn't* want him. Because she still had so much thinking to do, still had to work out how she had managed to give her heart to a guy who had no intention of looking after it—not in the long term and not, if she were to be honest with herself, in the short term either.

'No—don't!' She tempered the sharpness of her reply

with a little laugh. 'I know you've had a pretty distracted time when it comes to work, and that you get a lot done early in the morning. I'm still very sleepy anyway.' She yawned on cue. 'So I shall try and grab a couple more hours...'

'Sex is very good for guaranteeing restful sleep...' He slid into the bed alongside her and eased her to face him, so that they were both on their sides, looking at one another, perfectly level.

'In which case you should get back to work,' Alexa told him crisply, although her firmness was somewhat undermined by the hand that was now lying between her legs, cupping her down there and moving ever so gently. 'You don't want to fall asleep on the job, do you?'

Theo sighed and reluctantly removed his hand. 'Unfortunately that's the last thing I can afford to do,' he conceded. 'Several million pounds rests on my making sure I stay awake on the job—at least for the next couple of hours...'

He swung his legs over the side of the bed and strolled back towards the desk and the blinking of his computer. When he glanced over his shoulder it was to see that she was on her side, turned away from him, her long hair hiding her face, doubtless on her way back to sleep.

It seemed peculiar that he was going to be marrying a woman who, in the normal scheme of things, would not have excited his interest—and even more peculiar that she had not only excited his interest, but that his interest was showing no signs of petering out just yet.

He wondered what the chances were of a continuing sexual relationship for the duration of their imposed marriage, but dismissed the idea before it had taken root.

He just didn't have it in him to ride the crest of physical attraction for longer than a couple of months, and he knew without the shadow of a doubt, that to sleep with her for any continued period of time would be a big mistake.

He had always been able to deal with broken hearts, but this was a special case. When he and Alexa parted company they would still see one another, because he would have shares in her family company and would, on occasion, be working alongside her father. Her father was a sociable man. There would be instances when he would be invited over for a meal—special occasions, some family do—and there would be instances when she would be there too.

The last thing he wanted was to find himself in the firing line for recriminations should she get more involved with him than necessary. The last thing he wanted was her broken heart. Because she wasn't a tough, sexually experienced woman of the world and her broken heart might not mend quite so easily.

He heard her soft, even breathing and frowned, because thinking of her suffering did something to him.

Which, he concluded, was all the more reason to make sure what they had ended before it could become a problem. No big deal for him, but he might have to gently guide her in the same direction, just to make sure…

Alexa, her thoughts all over the place, actually fell asleep, and woke to the sound of her mobile buzzing next to her on the bedside table.

She could hear the sound of the shower in the bathroom. Predictably, the bathroom door was wide open, because Theo was anything but a shrinking violet when it came to flaunting his nudity.

It was her father, and their conversation was brief and puzzling. She waited until Theo was back in the bedroom, his hair damp and tousled and a towel hooked precariously around his waist.

'That was my dad…' She looked at him anxiously.

'What did he want?'

'He said that he has something to tell me but I'm not to

worry.' She sat up, heels tucked beneath her rear, and she chewed at her lip.

Being told not to worry was the fastest way to make sure that someone got worried—especially when it came to her father, who was the master of understatement.

Had her mother's health scare not been quite as severe as it had been, Alexa was sure that her father would have not deemed it necessary to contact her and ask her to return to Italy sixteen months ago. She'd been protected and sheltered as a child and that was the way it remained.

'What if something's wrong with Mum?' she asked in a quiet, wobbly voice.

Theo crossed over to the bed and looked at her uncertainly for a few seconds. The Alexa he had first met had changed over the brief but intense time they had spent together. Having expected a frumpy little doormat, he had been presented with a firebrand...

A feisty, outspoken, mutinous firebrand, who was also a ridiculous romantic...

Who had been a virgin...

He could sense her making a big effort not to cry, and he fought against his instinct to bracingly tell her to pull herself together.

'He'd tell you,' Theo informed her calmly. 'When it comes to health, people tend to avoid beating around the bush.'

'You don't know my father,' Alexa said ruefully. She suddenly realised that she wasn't wearing anything, and she hurriedly dragged the duvet over her and slumped back against the pillows.

'Fill me in.'

Alexa paused. This was what it meant to be in love, she thought. She could no more fight the urge to confide in him than a starving man could have fought the urge to feast at the banquet. Her head was telling her one thing—telling her to protect herself and back away—but she was drawn to him like a moth to the flame that threatened to kill it.

Being in love meant waving goodbye to common sense—to everything that had been her compass through her life.

'He's always hated the thought of worrying me,' she confessed. 'They wanted more kids, you know, but Mum had a terrible time when she was pregnant with me and was told that to risk having another would be endangering her life.' Alexa sighed. 'You could say that I've lived a pretty sheltered life. Not that I wasn't allowed out of their sight, but I was always protected from what they considered *too much information*. I only found out just how bad Mum's stroke was by cornering the consultant and demanding the details. Left to Dad, he would just have tutted and told me that everything was going to be fine. Which is why for him to call me here and say that he's got something to tell me... Well...'

Theo sat down on the bed, and she toppled a little towards him before steadying herself. For once he was with a woman, in a bed, and sex was not uppermost in his mind.

'I can only think that he's readying me for something big—that it's serious. And the only serious thing I can think of is that Mum... Well...'

Unaccustomed to soothing crying women, Theo pulled her towards him and smoothed her hair clumsily with his hand. She was crying against his chest but trying hard to stifle it, and that more than anything else touched him.

He hadn't had to dig too deep to find the soft-as-mush girl beneath the tough, outspoken exterior. And that was something he felt he should have sensed from the very beginning.

'So chewing over it and coming up with lots of worst-case scenarios...is that going to alter the reality?'

'Well, no...'

'If your mother was seriously ill your father would tell you—however much he didn't want to worry you—and if *he* wouldn't, then my father would call me and say something. You forget—they're back in touch now. And my father, I assure you, has *never* been backward when it comes to being brutally honest...'

'What do you mean?'

She was feeling better already. She liked the way he was holding her—as if she were a piece of fragile porcelain china. It felt good to be held like this, without sex being their final destination. It scared her how much she liked it...

'That art teacher might have been a bit forthright with Daniel,' Theo joked lightly, 'and I may have passed the litmus test with her by painting nonsense and talking my way into an explanation, but I remember my father taking one look at one of my productions and bursting out laughing. He said that it was the biggest load of rubbish he had ever seen, and then he patted me on the shoulder and told me that if *he* couldn't give me a few home truths then who could? So rest assured that he wouldn't shy away from phoning me if there was a crisis over there...'

'And has he?'

Theo looked at her with a frown. 'Has he what? Phoned me? To tell me about a crisis with your family? No.'

Alexa breathed a sigh of relief—because she believed him. It was as simple as that. She would wait and see what the problem was when she returned. Hopefully it would be something to do with the wedding or the engagement party.

Which brought her back to the thoughts that had momentarily taken a back seat.

She edged away from him and shuffled out of bed. Just now, knowing what she knew about her feelings for him, she felt that a bit of distance between them would be a good idea.

'So...' she said, gathering herself. 'It's our last day...'

She was well and truly up and awake now, and the thought of trying to pretend to go back to sleep wasn't going to work.

What happened next? she wondered.

The longer she carried on having sex with him, the more hurt she would be building up for herself. But how on earth was she going to last a year of wanting him and having to hide that want? How was she going to survive when he looked at her with polite indifference because what had started as lust for him had dwindled and disappeared?

The stakes were never going to be even between them, and just thinking about that made her head ache.

More than anything else she wished she could run away and take cover until this crazy love had blown over—except she knew that it never would.

She might no longer be able to keep her heart intact, but she felt she could try and keep her dignity intact—and to do so she would have to guard her expression and never allow him to see just how much he had finally ended up getting to her.

She wondered if this was the fate that had befallen all those women he had dated in the past. Having heard him give them his warning speech about not getting involved, had they, like her, found themselves being sucked into something that was bigger than them?

Had that been the fate of the striking blonde who had confronted him in that restaurant?

Alexa could only hope that, however hard she had fallen for him, she wouldn't be one of those women who kept trying to grab his attention whenever they happened to bump into him—who let him think that what he had once taken from them was still on offer should he decide to pay them another visit.

She had seen the way he had looked at that blonde, with

veiled contempt in his eyes—the same contempt that had been in his voice when he had talked about her.

There was no way Alexa would allow herself to become someone like that.

'I think we should do some sightseeing,' she said lightly. 'I'll just grab a shower and then we can think about heading out...maybe have breakfast at one of those bagel places by the hotel... Or we could go to Central Park... There's still so much to see... The earlier we leave, the better, don't you think?'

Theo inclined his head to one side, his antennae picking up invisible signals and trying to decipher them. 'Don't rush,' he told her with a little shrug, 'I'll have to wrap up these documents. It'll take at least half an hour...'

Alexa took longer than that, and emerged fully dressed an hour later. Theo, likewise, was in a pair of black jeans and a cream polo shirt that did amazing things for his athletic, muscular body.

She licked her lips and tried not to stare. Staring had been permissible when it had been about lust. Now that it was about love, staring was a weakness she could not afford.

Her heart was still beating fast and she frantically wondered how she could carry on sounding normal when everything inside her felt so *abnormal.*

She need not have worried. Theo's charm and the breadth of his knowledge proved irresistible.

She had, of course, travelled—but not nearly as extensively as he had, and he didn't allow her to be introspective as they had breakfast in a noisy bagel café before jumping on the subway—something she had to persuade him into doing—so that they could explore Williamsburg.

At one point he grabbed her hand and continued holding it. She knew that it was just one of those throwaway gestures of his, but also knew that would be one more thing she would store in her memory bank, to be extracted for examination at a later date.

She couldn't resist.

And she couldn't resist when he pulled her towards him and casually dropped a kiss on her parted lips.

She couldn't resist the way he took it for granted that her body belonged to him. Every passing touch was like the heavy brand of possession, but if he'd known the effect he had on her he would have been quailing at the thought of their year-long pretend union.

She hoped she'd kept everything on a light level, and by the time they'd headed back to the hotel and begun packing for their trip back to Italy she even managed to ask the question that had been uppermost in her mind for the past few hours.

'Should we discuss how we…er…move forward now…?'

About to fling the last of his clothing into his suitcase, Theo paused and stared at her. Something was off, but he couldn't quite put his finger on it.

'Come again?'

'Well, the week is up,' Alexa pointed out nervously. 'And I know that was the time limit we both agreed for us to…er…get this thing between us out of our system…'

'I don't recall agreeing to any such thing,' Theo pointed out.

She had come to him a virgin and yet now it seemed that she was keen to draw her experiences with him to a close. He clenched his jaw as it was brought home to him how little they had in common, aside from the obvious bond of their similar backgrounds, and how much, fundamentally, she still disapproved of him. He had the feeling that he'd been used, and it wasn't a feeling that he liked.

His cell phone buzzed and a text message popped up, saying that their limo had arrived to take them to the airport.

She had certainly started a tricky conversation at the

right point in time, he thought drily. Did she think that he would be too embarrassed to continue in the back of a taxi?

'Taxi's here,' he said curtly.

He phoned through to Reception to ask for their bags to be taken down to the limo and then waited until they were inside the spacious car before he picked up their conversation.

'Well…I know we didn't *exactly* set a time and a date,' Alexa said, when he lazily asked her to finish what she had started saying. 'I mean, I do understand that it's hard… impossible…'

'To set a time and a date when it comes to lust?' he interrupted smoothly. 'You're right. It is.'

'But,' she persisted valiantly, 'I do think we need some kind of clarification here…'

'Why?'

They did. He knew that. However, for some reason he had a perverse desire to dig his heels in. He wasn't ready to give up what they had, and there was nothing worse than unfinished business, as far as he was concerned.

True, when it came to women that was pure conjecture, but he couldn't see the point of self-denial and that was precisely the road she was trying to head down right now.

'Because this marriage of ours isn't going to be real,' Alexa mumbled. 'And if it's a business arrangement—'

'You can try.'

'I beg your pardon?'

'You can try to fight this thing between us, but you won't be getting any help from me.'

'What—what do you mean?' Alexa stammered.

'I mean that I'm not ready for this to end yet. And don't forget—we may have had a little respite from the cameras but we're heading back into the lions' den, and with our engagement those pesky reporters are going to be snapping away to capture the happy couple. I just want you to know that when I kiss you it won't be for the cameras...'

'I'd forgotten about them,' Alexa said in dismay.

He grinned wolfishly at her. 'Don't worry. It'll soon come flooding back...'

'So in other words,' Alexa said tightly, 'you want this to carry on until *you* get tired of it?'

'In other words, I have no intention of fighting what's between us.'

The taxi ride was completed in silence. Typically, Alexa thought, he had said what he had to say and then, rather than continue driving his point home, had dismissed the topic by spending the ride to the airport with his laptop open, sifting through dozens of emails and ignoring her completely.

He was just so damned *sure* of himself—just so *convinced* of his own monumental appeal that he didn't envisage her standing a chance of saying *no* to him.

She despaired.

Would she be able to withstand an onslaught? Even though she knew that he was not in it for more than just sex? Even though she knew that she would end up being desperately hurt? That she would turn into one of those clingy, needy women he had no time for? The sort who never forgot him and staged scenes whenever their paths chanced to cross?

All her resentment and anger, her conviction that she could never in a thousand years fall for a guy like him, now seemed like naïve stupidity. She had been able to hate the one-dimensional cardboard cut-out, but the minute the three-dimensional man had emerged she had not been able to resist.

She'd turned into just another one of his conquests, and she shivered at the prospect of those lips touching hers and her knowing that she wanted more. She was terrified of being betrayed—not just by her own weak body, but by her emotions.

Her head buzzed with so many scenarios that she was barely aware of the flight. He left her to stew. In fact she was certain that he wasn't even aware of her presence next to him. He was utterly absorbed in his work, and sex, however compelling, played second fiddle.

Only as they were taxiing on landing, and after having fitfully dozed for part of the trip, did she find other concerns settling—and the main one was whatever it might be that her father had to say to her.

All over again she felt anxiety begin to claw at her insides. Theo had calmed her fears by telling her that if her mother's health was involved *he* would have known about it. Now, Alexa could see all the flaws in that argument. Why would her father advertise something like that to his dad? It was a personal problem and he would surely want to keep it to himself. The fact that his instincts had always been to protect her from anything unpleasant meant that whatever he wanted to say must be of grave concern. It must be something he couldn't keep from her.

'What if something's really wrong with Mum?' she couldn't help asking as they disembarked.

She hated herself for appealing to Theo for reassurance, but she had had time to contemplate the worst and she *needed* to hear the strong conviction in his voice. It was irritating—especially considering she should be trying to erect whatever fragile defences she still had at her disposal to protect her pathetic, foolish heart—but she needed his logical explanation. Even though she had already convinced herself that it made no sense.

'It won't be.'

Theo had had plenty of time on the trip to try and work out why he was in the process of breaking his own self-imposed rule never to chase any woman. She was backing away, and instead of shrugging his shoulders and moving on he was intent on pursuit. Ego and pride, he presumed. Not exactly the most endearing traits in the world, but he wasn't going to pretend that there was anything more to it than that.

'But you don't *know*...'

Theo stared down at her flushed, earnest face and his libido kicked into gear with surprising ferocity. What *was* it about this woman that made him want to drag her off to the nearest empty room and take her?

He actually caught himself doing a brief mental tour of what he could recall of their route towards Immigration, trying to figure out if there were any cubbyholes he could pull her into, so that he could yank down those oh, so prim and proper trousers, taking her underwear with them, and have sex with her in the most basic way possible.

Reluctantly he gave up the idea, but this, he thought, was precisely why he would carry on his pursuit... Because to back off now, when neither of them wanted to, whatever she said to the contrary, would be like having to endure an indefinite erection without the benefit of a cold shower to get rid of it.

'Nor do you,' he said with a hint of impatience. 'Now, don't forget that we're back in the public eye. Try not to trail behind me—and it would help if you wiped that anxious expression off your face.'

With his free hand he massaged the nape of her neck, underneath her silky hair—which Alexa knew was unnecessary because there was no one with a camera around. But he had warned her that he wasn't going to play by her rules... He was just proving to her that he had meant what he said.

And right now, in these crowds, she was powerless to do anything about it.

Even when they were in the back of his chauffer-driven

car—he had called from the airport for it to come for them—she still had an insane urge to close the gap she had studiously put between them.

Like a predator, with all the time in the world to hunt its prey, he made no move to get closer to her, contenting himself with watching her through brooding, speculative eyes that gave her goosebumps.

Finally she hissed, with one eye on the driver, although the screen, as always, was up, 'I wish you'd stop staring at me!'

'Why?' Theo drawled.

'Because I don't like it!'

'Liar. You like it—and so do I.'

His words floated around her like a physical caress. There was lazy intent in his eyes and she looked away hurriedly, her body turned on to screaming point. Because he was one hundred per cent right... *She did like him staring at her—liked the way it made her whole body tingle, as though it had been plugged into an electric socket...*

She heard herself launch into nervous chatter, babbling even while her body recalled how and where it had been touched, and fought against the seductive temptation to think about how and where it would be touched again...

She was surprised that they made it to her house with her nervous system still intact. Of course he hadn't opened his computer once, or checked his phone at all. He'd just leaned against the door, limbs loose, his fabulous green eyes pinned to her face, fully aware that he was unsettling her and amused by it.

'I'll come in with you,' Theo murmured, pressing a button and talking to the driver once the partition was lowered.

'There's no need,' Alexa said hastily.

He didn't bother to answer, instead stepping out of the car and moving round to wait for her as she followed suit.

'There's no need to pretend now that we're here,' she muttered as he neatly tucked her arm into the crook of his.

'Oh, I know *that*,' Theo murmured silkily, 'but remember what I said to you?'

Alexa's breath caught in her throat, because she knew that she just didn't have the weapons for a sustained assault.

'And remember what *I* said to *you*!' But her voice was weak.

He actually laughed under his breath. Laughed and patted her on her arm. 'You want me. Don't fight it, Alexa. Enjoy it while it lasts. Now...' his tone changed from lazy to brisk as he rang the doorbell '...why don't we see what all the fuss is about with your father?'

CHAPTER TEN

NOT ONLY WAS her father waiting for her, so was her mother. And, even more ominous, so was Theo's father. All three were hovering by the door, and she got the uneasy feeling that they had been waiting for their arrival.

Alexa automatically stepped a shade closer to Theo, who had sized up the situation and taken charge, smoothly querying their joint presence by the front door with the quirk of an eyebrow but not commenting on it, instead leading the way into the kitchen while conducting a running commentary on their trip, omitting the salacious details and focusing on filling his father in on Bob and Felicity.

They followed him like sheep.

The man was a born leader, and she could understand why her father had dangled the carrot of shares in the family firm, ensuring that he would oversee holding its reins in the years to come. A true marriage of convenience.

'So...'

Somehow, without her noticing, Theo had managed to pour their collected parents glasses of wine and put the kettle on for coffee for both of them. He sauntered towards the kitchen table, which was a long oak affair that could comfortably seat twelve. He looked perfectly relaxed and utterly in charge.

'Which lucky family member gets to tell us what's

going on…?' he drawled, patting the chair next to him, into which Alexa sank with a sigh of relief, because nervous tension at this new, unsettling situation had piled up on top of the nervous tension already wreaking havoc inside her. He looked narrowly from face to face and his father cleared his throat.

'We have been talking, son—' Stefano said, sitting at the head of the table while the other two followed suit, flanking him on either side. Alexa's mother nervously twirled the stem of her wine glass and looked at her daughter,

'Let *me*, Stefano,' Cora interrupted. 'Now, Alexa, your father's come clean and told me everything. I know you two have been worried sick about me, and I understand that you reached this…this…*arrangement* with poor Theo for the best possible reasons, but I don't need protecting as much as you think.'

She looked lovingly at her husband, who looked away sheepishly.

Alexa's brain had stopped at the description of Theo as 'poor', as in *helpless*, and she wanted to burst into hysterical laughter.

'I've had health problems, all three of you know that, but they've been physical—not emotional. Yes, I'll admit that I may have told your father, Alexa, that I longed for a grandchild—longed to see you settled down with a nice man—but what mother doesn't wish that for her child? There was no need for you to concoct this silly scheme…'

'So what are you saying?' Alexa looked between the three parents in bewilderment. She was trying to follow what her mother was saying, but it was like walking in treacle. When she looked at Theo he was frowning, his brooding eyes speculative. It hit her just how much she had come to admire the silent strength of his personality, and was floored by how much it hurt to love him when her love wasn't returned.

Stefano picked up the thread of the conversation. 'We're saying that there's no need for this charade any longer. Certain things will remain in place...'

'I promised you shares in my company,' Carlo said, addressing Theo, 'and that stays in place. I won't pretend that I didn't...' he cleared his throat '...see certain advantages to helping your father out financially...'

'Because you're a manipulative old man.' Cora smiled indulgently at her husband. 'But, Alexa, darling, I don't understand why you didn't put your foot down and refuse to go through with this silly pretence. No...' She sighed. 'I *do* understand, and for that I have only love for you...'

Alexa's head was swimming. She was now grasping exactly what was being said. She had been looking at the prospect of a year with Theo—a year trying to fight the impulses that were so much bigger than her...a year knowing that every time he crooked his finger it would take all the strength at her disposal not to go running...a year of knowing that she would walk away from their relationship battered and hurt beyond comprehension.

That year wasn't going to happen now. She was being given her *Get Out Of Jail Free* card—and so was Theo.

And the future yawned in front of her like a black, empty void.

'So...' she said slowly.

'Yes, my darling.' Cora reached across the width of the kitchen table to pat her daughter's hand. 'And of course the press have hounded you both. You will simply tell them that the engagement's off and so is the marriage...'

Alexa headed for the most secluded seat in the first class lounge at the airport. She didn't want to be near anyone because she didn't want to be dragged into making small talk. She'd been operating on automatic for the past three weeks and she planned on carrying on doing just that—at least until she reached London, when she was banking on new surroundings and the thrill of her new job to rescue her from the zombie-like torpor into which she had sunk.

Where had Theo gone? She didn't know, and of course she had been too proud to ask her parents. She had moaned and railed against the situation in which she had found herself, and yet when that situation had been whipped out from under her feet she had been lost because she had become so dependent on him.

In the blink of an eye he had gone from being just the sort of guy she would run a mile from to being just the sort of guy she couldn't imagine living without.

But live without him she would, and it hurt more than she could ever have contemplated in those carefree first few days when she had actually disliked him.

The press, predictably, had passed a few days speculating on the break-up of the perfectly matched couple and then, just as predictably, new scandals and gossip had drawn them away.

Now, staring down at the book on her lap, and with two hours of waiting ahead of her because she had been itching to leave, she thought back to the brief conversation she had had with Theo after his father and her parents had fled the scene, leaving them stranded in the kitchen like a couple of castaways, washed up on a beach after being stuck on a raft together but with nothing to say now that the storm had passed.

The passionate lover had gone. He had carefully asked her what her plans were now. One minute he hadn't been able to keep his hands off her—the next minute, freed from the shackles of a union he'd never asked for, he'd been coolly indifferent.

Of course *she* had gone on about the relief of not having to face a marriage neither of them had wanted. The more indifferent he'd seemed, the more she had sparkled, voicing the joys of her newfound freedom.

And then he'd gone, and she'd been left in an empty kitchen contemplating the horror of her newfound freedom.

London. Her parents had an apartment there. It was where she had lived before she had left for Italy and she would go back there. She had phoned her old company, who had remembered her, and after a million calls they had found her a job.

The change of scene would do her good—she knew that. Just being in her parents' house had reminded her of Theo. And in the dead of night, her whole body ached for him.

Right, she thought severely, *think about the good stuff.*

No falling deeper and deeper in love with a man who didn't love her. No agonising year together, during which time he would have grown tired of her body and settled back into enduring the time he was forced to spend in her company. He had simply been her lover, and she knew that she would eventually meet someone else—someone she could entrust with her heart.

She forced herself to read a few pages of her book and was totally unaware of anyone approaching her until a shadow fell over her. When she looked down she saw a pair of very expensive loafers and didn't bother to look any higher, because if she didn't then whoever it was wouldn't ask her if she'd mind if he sat next to her.

'Alexa.'

For a few seconds Alexa was convinced that she'd misheard her name being said—and had definitely misconstrued that rich, mellow voice she had come to love.

She hunkered down and ignored whoever it was—because he *hadn't* spoken, and it was just her feverish imagination playing tricks on her.

'Are you going to acknowledge me or are you going to carry on reading...? What are you reading?'

The book was whipped out of her hands and there he was, standing right in front of her, as cool as a cucumber and as devastatingly sexy as every single memory she had of him.

In a pair of cream trousers and a black T-shirt, with a cream linen jacket hooked over one shoulder, he was drop-dead gorgeous.

'Still on the crime novels, I see. Would you like me to predict the end?'

'What are you doing here?'

Her voice was a hoarse whisper and she cleared her throat, then fidgeted as he took the empty chair next to her and pulled it in, so that there was no way she could avoid looking at him.

Theo wished there was an easy answer to that question— something glib that he could pull out from up his sleeve— but there wasn't. He had spent the past three weeks unable to focus, unable to concentrate—unable to do anything but think about her, even though he had told himself that it was great that he had been released from the obligation of a marriage he hadn't wanted...great that he could resume his life as he had always wanted it...great that his routine would be returned to him.

His address book was bulging with names and phone numbers of women, and all of them without exception would have welcomed a call from him. He had known that.

He hadn't called any of them because he'd had too much catching up to do on the work front. That was what he had told himself. Until he'd been forced to face the fact that he missed *her*. Not just her warm, welcoming body, which he had known for such a brief period of time, but he missed the whole package. He missed the way she bristled and glared at him...the way she never obeyed any of his 'No

Trespassing' signs but got stuck in and told him just what she thought of him anyway. He missed her shy, hesitant smiles and the ready way her eyes filled up with tears. He missed the softness underneath the feisty scrapper. Most of all he just missed the woman who had been born to have it all and had chosen to do her own thing and ignore the life she had been conditioned to lead.

Except he had no idea how to put any of that into words, and he could feel her blazing eyes on him—could feel her willing him to just *go away.*

'How have you been?' he asked, in a lame attempt to kick-start the conversation.

'Fine,' Alexa said coldly. 'Are you travelling to London? I had no idea.'

'And if you had you would have checked on to a different flight...?'

Alexa shrugged. 'Probably,' she told him truthfully. 'You can't deny that this situation is a little uncomfortable at the moment. I do realise we'll probably bump into one another in the years to come, but right now...'

'I get it. From being lovers and engaged to...nothing...'

Resting his forearms on his thighs as he leaned forward, Theo raked his fingers through his hair and took some small comfort from the delicate blush that bloomed in her cheeks at the mention of their having been lovers.

'I don't want to talk about that,' Alexa said stiffly. 'In fact I'd rather you left me alone,' she continued, barely able to look at him. 'I have lots of planning to do for my new job in London and I really would like to do that in peace and quiet.'

'No.'

Alexa's mouth dropped open and she stared at him. 'What do you mean, *no*?' she demanded furiously.

'I haven't come here so that I can disappear without telling you what I've come to say.'

'Which is what?'

'I liked being engaged to you.' He looked around him at the crowded lounge. 'I have my driver outside.'

'I *beg* your pardon?'

Alexa was frantically trying to analyse what he had just said about liking being engaged to her. What did *that* mean? She didn't want to dwell on it, because it meant nothing coming from a man who had spent the past three weeks avoiding her and who didn't have a committed bone in his body—a man who had a block of ice for a heart.

'I want to talk to you and I can't do it here.'

'Well, *I* don't want to talk to *you*.' Alexa's body was ramrod-straight and as stiff as a board. She dreaded that one of those hands loosely dangling between his thighs might accidentally brush against her, because if it did then she knew the already uphill task of projecting indifference would be even harder.

'Please.'

That single word was wrenched out of him and for a second she hesitated, because *please* was not a word that passed his lips very often.

'What do you want to talk about?' she asked, relenting a little.

Theo glanced at her and kept his gaze on her face.

'I've missed you,' he said roughly, and Alexa tried to hold on to some of her gritty determination not to melt.

You've missed having sex with me.

'Are you travelling to London as well?'

'I will if I have to. I'm booked on the same flight as you, although I'd rather we didn't have this conversation on a plane or in an airport lounge...'

'Look, I can't think that there's anything to talk about, Theo. I mean, you've got your freedom, and I know that was all you wanted when you thought you'd lost it for a year. So maybe you miss having sex with me? You said that you wanted to carry on sleeping with me until… Well, until you got bored and dispatched me to wherever it is you dispatch women you no longer want hanging around. Some locked cupboard in your head, I expect. Of course, physically I'd have still been around, until the year ran out, but as far as sleeping with me went I guess it would have been separate rooms and you discreetly returning to your diet of leggy blonde supermodels…'

Her voice was brittle and she looked away and stared straight ahead.

'So I'm not going to jump into bed with you again just because you're not bored with me yet, Theo.'

Theo heard what she was saying and knew that she was describing the man he had thought himself to be. Even when they had walked away from one another he had still thought himself to be a guy who worked hard, played hard and avoided commitment.

'And I wouldn't ask you to,' he said quietly. 'Are you sure you won't dump your flight so that we can have this conversation somewhere a little less…frantic?'

'No one's paying us a scrap of attention.' She sighed with heartfelt longing. 'I just want to get to London and begin a new chapter in my life.'

Theo's jaw hardened. He had heard a lot about this wonderful new chapter in her life on the night they had returned from the best time he had ever had with a woman, to discover that the charade was over and they were free to go. She couldn't have waxed more lyrical when it had come to letting him know how relieved she was that the pretence was over.

Pride had turned his responses then to ice, and pride had kept him away for three weeks, but now he had discovered that there was something more powerful than pride and that had been a bitter pill to swallow.

'Your mother tells me that you have a new job lined up.'

'You spoke to her?'

'That's how I knew that you would be leaving for London today. She told me a few days ago...'

'*A few days ago?* Since when have you and my mother been having cosy chats behind my back? She never mentioned a word about talking to you!'

'Because I asked her not to.' Theo flushed darkly.

'You *asked her not to*? Why would you do that?' Alexa was genuinely bewildered.

'I...' He hunkered down.

Never in his life had he felt less cool, more in danger of making a complete fool of himself and more exposed to rejection. Indeed, when it came to women he had *never* felt exposed to rejection, and he loathed the feeling of vulnerability. He had never been vulnerable. He had always had the direction of his life firmly within his controlling hand.

Alexa was even more bewildered at his discomfort. It just wasn't *him*.

'I never thought I wanted involvement with a woman,' Theo surprised her by saying. His eyes met hers and held them. 'Don't interrupt me,' he continued, returning to some of his usual form. 'I...I didn't have any crash-and-burn relationships that turned me off commitment. I never lost my heart to a gold-digger only to find out in the nick of time. I suppose I was simply a product of my background—just as my brother is. I was ambitious, and in my upward climb I enjoyed women but never invited any of them further than the front door, emotionally speaking.'

Alexa gave him an encouraging look. She was all ears.

'I was in no hurry to settle down—in fact it never crossed my mind what sort of woman I would end up with, or even if I would end up with one at all.' He paused and thought about the relationship his parents had had. 'When my mother died Daniel and I watched my father fall apart at the seams. Actually,' he confessed heavily, 'we *all* fell apart. And that was when I realised just how destructive all-consuming love can be.'

'Empowering,' Alexa corrected in a staccato voice. 'I'm sure your father would agree that it was better to have had all those wonderful years with your mother than to have lived the sort of life *you* want to carve out for yourself.'

Theo smiled crookedly at her. 'And that's why I thought that, whether I married you or not, you and I were poles apart. I admit that the only kind of marriage that ever crossed my mind after my mother died was one that would have been very similar to the one we found ourselves pushed into—a marriage of convenience. But not with a woman who was all about romance and love and happy-ever-after endings... What I anticipated was a relationship where I couldn't be hurt—a relationship that was a mutually convenient business arrangement...'

'So you've come here to tell me what I already knew?'

'No. I've come here to tell you that I was wrong.'

Hope flared inside her, suffocating everything else and shooting up blooms that she couldn't squash.

'What do you mean?' Alexa asked in a stifled voice.

'You *know* what I mean,' Theo said drily. 'I was wrong. I might have *wanted* a relationship I could control, but in the end I *needed* the relationship that I couldn't. I needed *you*. I still do...'

Alexa masked her disappointment, because need was very far from love. 'And that's why you're not the man for me,' she said softly. 'You've learned to be cynical and I've learned the opposite. I don't want something that stops at *need* or *desire* or *lust*. I want the full package and I always did.'

'And why can't that be *me*?' Theo demanded with muted belligerence.

He had never had to justify how he felt to anyone in his

life before, and even if he left now, without her, he was driven to lay himself open to that possibility.

'Because—'

'I love you, Alexa. I never expected to, but somehow it just…happened. Without even realising it I let you into my life, and I came here to tell you that I don't want you to leave it. I came here to ask you if you'd be mine for ever. Hell, Alexa, I came here to propose to you now that we're no longer engaged…'

'You *love* me…?'

The words hitched in her throat and she tentatively stroked his knuckles with her finger, wishing now that she had abandoned her flight and gone somewhere else with him for this conversation—but how was she supposed to have known what he had come to say?

'You have no idea how much I've longed to hear you say that,' she whispered tremulously. 'I didn't think I would ever fall in love with you. You didn't make sense. I'd always assumed that the guy I fell for would be…well, just the *opposite* of you, to be honest. And I hated it that I was being forced into marrying you…'

'Tell me about it. I've never known a woman fight me as much as you did…'

Alexa laughed. She believed him. She'd dug her heels in. But even when she'd thought that she was refusing to budge an inch more than necessary she had already been shifting in places she hadn't begun to understand.

'I was so desperate for you to be the horrible, arrogant person I wanted you to be, but it felt like with every day that passed you escaped the box I'd shoved you in just a little bit more—until I realised that I'd fallen in love with the three-dimensional guy I never thought you could ever be.' She frowned as a sudden thought occurred to her. 'Did you tell my mother why you were coming here?'

'It was the only way I could find out what sort of reception I might expect,' he confessed, with such humility that she wanted to kiss him and keep right on kissing him. 'I swore her to secrecy,' he further admitted. 'She was to say nothing if it turned out that you wanted me out of your life for good.'

'I love you so much, Theo,' Alexa whispered, half giggling, because this was such an inappropriate place for such a wildly wonderful marriage proposal.

'So you'll marry me...?'

'Try and stop me...'

* * * * *

If you enjoyed reading Theo's story,
you'll love his brother Daniel's:
THE SURPRISE DE ANGELIS BABY
Coming next month!

MILLS & BOON®
Hardback – January 2016

ROMANCE

The Queen's New Year Secret	Maisey Yates
Wearing the De Angelis Ring	Cathy Williams
The Cost of the Forbidden	Carol Marinelli
Mistress of His Revenge	Chantelle Shaw
Theseus Discovers His Heir	Michelle Smart
The Marriage He Must Keep	Dani Collins
Awakening the Ravensdale Heiress	Melanie Milburne
New Year at the Boss's Bidding	Rachael Thomas
His Princess of Convenience	Rebecca Winters
Holiday with the Millionaire	Scarlet Wilson
The Husband She'd Never Met	Barbara Hannay
Unlocking Her Boss's Heart	Christy McKellen
A Daddy for Baby Zoe?	Fiona Lowe
A Love Against All Odds	Emily Forbes
Her Playboy's Proposal	Kate Hardy
One Night...with Her Boss	Annie O'Neil
A Mother for His Adopted Son	Lynne Marshall
A Kiss to Change Her Life	Karin Baine
Twin Heirs to His Throne	Olivia Gates
A Baby for the Boss	Maureen Child

MILLS & BOON®
Large Print – January 2016

ROMANCE

The Greek Commands His Mistress	Lynne Graham
A Pawn in the Playboy's Game	Cathy Williams
Bound to the Warrior King	Maisey Yates
Her Nine Month Confession	Kim Lawrence
Traded to the Desert Sheikh	Caitlin Crews
A Bride Worth Millions	Chantelle Shaw
Vows of Revenge	Dani Collins
Reunited by a Baby Secret	Michelle Douglas
A Wedding for the Greek Tycoon	Rebecca Winters
Beauty & Her Billionaire Boss	Barbara Wallace
Newborn on Her Doorstep	Ellie Darkins

HISTORICAL

Marriage Made in Shame	Sophia James
Tarnished, Tempted and Tamed	Mary Brendan
Forbidden to the Duke	Liz Tyner
The Rebel Daughter	Lauri Robinson
Her Enemy Highlander	Nicole Locke

MEDICAL

Unlocking Her Surgeon's Heart	Fiona Lowe
Her Playboy's Secret	Tina Beckett
The Doctor She Left Behind	Scarlet Wilson
Taming Her Navy Doc	Amy Ruttan
A Promise...to a Proposal?	Kate Hardy
Her Family for Keeps	Molly Evans

1215 GEN STD LP

MILLS & BOON®
Hardback – February 2016

ROMANCE

Leonetti's Housekeeper Bride	Lynne Graham
The Surprise De Angelis Baby	Cathy Williams
Castelli's Virgin Widow	Caitlin Crews
The Consequence He Must Claim	Dani Collins
Helios Crowns His Mistress	Michelle Smart
Illicit Night with the Greek	Susanna Carr
The Sheikh's Pregnant Prisoner	Tara Pammi
A Deal Sealed by Passion	Louise Fuller
Saved by the CEO	Barbara Wallace
Pregnant with a Royal Baby!	Susan Meier
A Deal to Mend Their Marriage	Michelle Douglas
Swept into the Rich Man's World	Katrina Cudmore
His Shock Valentine's Proposal	Amy Ruttan
Craving Her Ex-Army Doc	Amy Ruttan
The Man She Could Never Forget	Meredith Webber
The Nurse Who Stole His Heart	Alison Roberts
Her Holiday Miracle	Joanna Neil
Discovering Dr Riley	Annie Claydon
His Forever Family	Sarah M. Anderson
How to Sleep with the Boss	Janice Maynard

MILLS & BOON®
Large Print – February 2016

ROMANCE

Claimed for Makarov's Baby — Sharon Kendrick
An Heir Fit for a King — Abby Green
The Wedding Night Debt — Cathy Williams
Seducing His Enemy's Daughter — Annie West
Reunited for the Billionaire's Legacy — Jennifer Hayward
Hidden in the Sheikh's Harem — Michelle Conder
Resisting the Sicilian Playboy — Amanda Cinelli
Soldier, Hero...Husband? — Cara Colter
Falling for Mr December — Kate Hardy
The Baby Who Saved Christmas — Alison Roberts
A Proposal Worth Millions — Sophie Pembroke

HISTORICAL

Christian Seaton: Duke of Danger — Carole Mortimer
The Soldier's Rebel Lover — Marguerite Kaye
Return of Scandal's Son — Janice Preston
The Forgotten Daughter — Lauri Robinson
No Conventional Miss — Eleanor Webster

MEDICAL

Hot Doc from Her Past — Tina Beckett
Surgeons, Rivals...Lovers — Amalie Berlin
Best Friend to Perfect Bride — Jennifer Taylor
Resisting Her Rebel Doc — Joanna Neil
A Baby to Bind Them — Susanne Hampton
Doctor...to Duchess? — Annie O'Neil

0116 GEN STD LP

MILLS & BOON®

Why shop at millsandboon.co.uk?

Each year, thousands of romance readers find their perfect read at millsandboon.co.uk. That's because we're passionate about bringing you the very best romantic fiction. Here are some of the advantages of shopping at www.millsandboon.co.uk:

* **Get new books first**—you'll be able to buy your favourite books one month before they hit the shops

* **Get exclusive discounts**—you'll also be able to buy our specially created monthly collections, with up to 50% off the RRP

* **Find your favourite authors**—latest news, interviews and new releases for all your favourite authors and series on our website, plus ideas for what to try next

* **Join in**—once you've bought your favourite books, don't forget to register with us to rate, review and join in the discussions

Visit **www.millsandboon.co.uk**
for all this and more today!